"I'm sorry you came all the way here, only to be disappointed."

"No, it's not about that," Dylan said. "It's just—"

Just what? How could he explain it to Holly without hurting her or making her feel more ashamed of the information she'd withheld? He needed to be sensitive to her feelings, but at the same time, he couldn't sugarcoat things.

He had to be honest with himself, as well as Holly.

"I suppose you had a preconceived notion about me, right?" she asked. "Cute. Blonde. Blue-eyed. Standing on two feet."

She breathed out a tiny huff of air. "Wheelchairs don't exactly come to mind when you're painting a picture in your head of someone, do they?"

He let out a ragged sigh, then raked his fingers through his military cut. "If I'd known from the beginning I'm sure I wouldn't be feeling this way. Okay, that's not true. Or maybe it is. I just feel a little caught off guard."

Where would they go from here?

Books by Belle Calhoune

Love Inspired

Reunited with the Sheriff
Forever Her Hero
Heart of a Soldier

BELLE CALHOUNE

was born and raised in Massachusetts. Some of her fondest childhood memories revolve around her four siblings and spending summers in Cape Cod. Although both her parents were in the medical field, she became an avid reader of romance novels as a teen and began dreaming of a career as an author. Shortly thereafter, she began writing her own stories. Married to her college sweetheart, she is raising two lovely daughters in Connecticut. A dog lover, she has a beautiful chocolate Lab and an adorable mini poodle. After studying French for ten years and traveling extensively throughout France, she considers herself a Francophile. When she's not writing, she enjoys spending time in Cape Cod and planning her next Parisian escape. She finds writing inspirational romance to be a joyful experience that nurtures her soul. You can write to her at scalhoune@gmail.com or contact her through her website, bellecalhoune.com.

Heart of a Soldier

Belle Calhoune

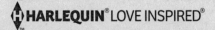
HARLEQUIN® LOVE INSPIRED®

Recycling programs
for this product may
not exist in your area.

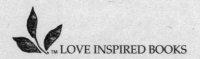

LOVE INSPIRED BOOKS

ISBN-13: 978-0-373-87935-9

Heart of a Soldier

Printed in U.S.A.

Delight yourself in the Lord and he will give you
the desires of your heart.
—*Psalms* 37:4

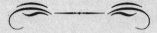

For my daughter Sierra.
I love your independence, creativity and wisdom.
You are beautiful inside and out, with the heart
and imagination of a writer. I love watching you
soar like an Eagle. Always remember there are
no limits to the things you can achieve.

Acknowledgments

For all my family and friends for all their support
and love, especially my Dad, my sister, Karen,
and my friend Lim Riley.

I owe a debt of gratitude to my editor, Emily Rodmell,
for catching all the things I tend to overlook
and for wholeheartedly embracing my heroine.

I am very grateful to all the readers who wrote to me
asking when I was going to write Holly's story.
Your enthusiasm inspired me to create
a love story worthy of all your expectations.

Chapter One

West Falls, Texas

Holly Lynch quickly made her way to the mailbox, parking her wheelchair next to it so she could scoop the mail out and place it in her lap. Once she'd dumped the mail onto her skirt, she riffled through it, a smile lighting up her face as she saw the familiar handwriting. She ripped the envelope open with her finger, pulling the crisp stationery out and lifting it to her nose to inhale the aroma. She closed her eyes and breathed in the woodsy, spicy scent. She imagined Dylan Hart smelled just like this piece of stationery, as clean and fresh as a pine tree. A photo fell out of the letter, landing on her lap, faceup. She stared down at Dylan—her gorgeous, green-eyed, smiling soldier—her heart doing flip-flops at the sight of him. He was dressed in his uniform and grinning into the camera, showcasing his impressive dimples and unforgettable face.

She opened the letter, noticing it was dated almost three weeks ago. This was how long it took to get a letter to and from Afghanistan. She let out a deep sigh. Three long weeks! A lifetime, as far as she was concerned. Her hands trembled as she began reading the letter.

Dear Holly,

I hope this letter finds you well. On this end, things couldn't be better.

My tour of duty came to an end a few weeks ago. I'm pleased to report that I've received an honorable discharge. Finally, at long last, I'm coming home for good. I arrive stateside on October 1. I'm spending some time with my mom and her new husband, Roy. She's been taking really good care of Leo for me while I've been in Afghanistan. Here's the really good part. I'm planning to come to West Falls on October 15. Sorry for not telling you sooner, but I wanted it to be a surprise.

I hope this is welcome news to you, Holly. We've been talking about our first meeting for so long now. I can hardly believe it's happening. By the time this letter reaches you, I'll almost be there, at your side.

There's so much more I want to say, words that can be said only face-to-face.

Until then, be safe.

Fondly,
Dylan

The letter slipped from Holly's fingers, floating down to the ground like a leaf falling from a tree. Its graceful descent belied the turmoil raging inside her. Dylan Hart, the pen pal she'd been corresponding with for a little over a year while he was stationed in Afghanistan, was coming to West Falls, all the way from Oklahoma to see her. And according to his letter, he'd be arriving sometime today. With mail scattered all over her lap, Holly adroitly maneuvered her wheelchair up the ramp leading to the front porch. She barreled her way inside the house and double locked the front door behind her. Once she was safely inside, she concentrated on breathing normally. She was taking in huge gulps of air, but she still felt as if she couldn't breathe. Her palms were sweaty, and beads of moisture had broken out on her forehead. The sound of her labored breathing thundered in her ears.

Dear Lord, help me. I don't know what to do. Please don't let Dylan come here!

Bingo, her chocolate Lab, padded his way to her side. Sensing her frantic mood, he cocked his head to the side, then began to gently lick her hand. Reaching out, she patted his head, looking deeply into his russet-colored eyes.

"Bingo, what am I going to do?" she asked as panic skittered through her.

She wanted to hide! She wanted to get in her van and drive as fast and far from Horseshoe Bend Ranch as possible. There was no way in the world she could face Dylan. Because as much as she adored him, as much as she ached to see those brilliant green eyes in person, she didn't have the courage to deal with this situation she'd created. She couldn't face the secret she'd kept from him. Somehow, in all the letters they'd exchanged, she'd failed to tell him the single most important fact about herself.

She was a paraplegic. She'd lost the use of her legs in an accident, and she'd never walk again. Not in this lifetime. Brave, handsome Dylan, who'd proudly served his country in Afghanistan, had no clue that the woman he'd been writing to—the woman he was traveling all this way to see—was not the woman he believed her to be.

Dylan Hart let out a low whistle as he pulled up in front of the Horseshoe Bend Ranch. In all his life he'd never seen anything finer. It made the Bar M back home seem like chopped liver. The massive entrance dwarfed him, making him feel insignificant in the scheme of things. As he drove past the gates, all he could see stretched out before him was lush green grass—acres upon acres of the purest horse land in the entire state.

Although Holly had told him her family owned a ranch and it had been in her family for generations, he hadn't been expecting anything this impressive. For a man who'd been just getting by for most of his life, it left him a little unsettled. Here he was, fresh from a combat zone, with nothing to offer Holly but his sincerity and the special friendship they'd both nurtured. He swallowed past the huge lump in his throat, hoping it was enough to land him the woman of his dreams.

He knew he was getting ahead of himself, but he couldn't help it. He had such a good feeling about Holly—she aroused emotions in him that he hadn't felt in a long time. It wasn't love—he wasn't that deep in— but something in his gut told him she could be the one.

While he'd been over in Afghanistan, there had been endless amounts of time to think about his future. When the bottom fell out of his world, everything had become crystal clear. A place to call home, a good woman by his side and a strong sense of community. More than anything else in the world, that was what he wanted.

And here he was in West Falls, Texas, taking a huge leap of faith. It wasn't like him, not even remotely, but here he stood, ready to embrace his future. Even though he didn't have a job lined up and this could all blow up in his face, he was willing to reach for the brass ring. He was prepared to put his painful past firmly in his rearview mirror. He was giving it his best shot.

Holly could be the one to make him forget about roadside bombs and friends who would never make it back home. She could be the one to make him believe that there were true, honest women out there in the world. And today he would be seeing her for the first time, since he didn't own a single picture of her. How he wanted to see those baby-blue eyes she'd described in person! He'd dreamed about meeting Holly for months now. Although excitement was building inside him, there was also a slight feeling of doubt. Was he doing the right thing?

Lord, please let this rash decision to come all the way to West Falls be right! Let Holly be the woman You've picked for me to fall in love with, something lasting and real. I'm so tired of doing this alone. I'm so afraid of ending up by myself.

After driving for about a half mile, he reached a fork in the road. He saw a grand home looming in the distance. As someone who loved architecture, he appreciated its beauty. It was the type of house that made a person sit up and take notice. It was an impressive two-story white structure with a long wraparound porch and shiny black shutters. It looked like the type of house he would have loved to have grown up in. This place, Dylan thought with amazement, was a far cry from the small trailer where he'd spent the first eighteen years of his life.

He parked his truck and got out, then made his way to the porch steps in a few easy strides. To the left of the stairs was a wheelchair-accessible ramp leading to the front porch. The sight of the bright red door had him grinning. It made the grand house look warm and inviting—the same way Holly had seemed in all her letters. Blue and red rocking chairs sat facing each other, just waiting, he imagined, for someone to plop down and sit for a spell.

He looked down at himself, hoping his favorite blue shirt and well-worn jeans made him look presentable. With a hint of impatience, he rang the doorbell, itching to meet his pen pal after all these days, weeks and months. Seconds later he rang it again, then knocked on the door for good measure. When no one answered after a few tense minutes, he rapped again on the door, this time with a little more force.

He heard something—or someone—inside the house. A rattling noise sounded by the door, and he heard a whirring sound. Every instinct he possessed told him that someone was in there. "Afternoon. I'm looking for Holly Lynch," he called out.

The heavy click of a lock being turned echoed in the stillness of the fall afternoon. With a slow creak, the door opened. A woman was there, sitting in a wheelchair, her blue eyes as wide as saucers. She had dirty-blond hair and a pretty face that gave her a girl-next-door look. A smattering of freckles crisscrossed her nose. Even though the blue eyes held a look of fear, they were beautiful. They reminded him of his mama's favorite flowers—cornflowers. A necklace with a diamond pendant hung around her neck. She was wearing a T-shirt that read I Do My Own Stunts. The shirt made him want to laugh out loud at her spunk and sense of humor.

The young lady was just sitting there, staring at him without saying a single word. Had he scared her that badly with his knocking and ringing the bell? She was looking at him as if he were the Big Bad Wolf ready to pounce on Little Red Riding Hood.

"Sorry to bother you, miss, but I'm looking for Holly." He extended a hand and grinned at her, wanting to take away some of her nervousness. "I'm Dylan Hart. A friend of Holly's."

Tentatively, she reached out and shook his hand, giving him a slight smile. The blue eyes still looked wary, and the half smile never quite made its way to her eyes. She folded her arms across her chest as if she was guarding herself against him. He wasn't sure if he was imagining things, but her posture looked downright uninviting.

"And you are?" he asked, leading her to introduce herself.

"C-Cassidy. I'm Cassidy Blake," she answered in a quiet voice.

Cassidy! Holly had written to him about her best

friend, Cassidy, who was engaged to Holly's brother, Tate. Holly had never once mentioned that Cassidy was in a wheelchair. Or had she? No, he wouldn't have forgotten something like that. Maybe Holly was so used to Cassidy's condition that she hadn't thought to mention it. It was a little bit shocking to see such a young woman confined to a wheelchair. He wondered what had happened to put her there.

"I just got into town a little while ago. Is Holly here?" He didn't want to be rude, but cutting to the chase was his style. He'd come all this way for Holly. Just one look in her eyes, and he knew all would feel right in his world.

Cassidy seemed to think for a moment before she answered him. "Um, no, she's not. She went into town to run a few errands. I don't think she was expecting you until later. She just received your letter today."

Dylan glanced at his watch. It was two o'clock. Something told him Cassidy wouldn't want him hanging around the house, waiting for Holly's return. She had a strange look on her face—somewhere between anxiety and horror.

"I guess I'll head back into town and unpack my things to kill some time," he said, wanting to fill the silence with a little conversation. He couldn't shake the sense that she was nervous about his being here. Hopefully she wasn't worried about her safety. As far as he knew, he looked fairly trustworthy, although anyone could be a stalker nowadays.

Her mouth swung open. "You're staying in town?"

"Yeah," he said with a smile. "I rented a small cottage right near Main Street. My landlord is Doc Sampson. He runs a restaurant in town."

"Yes, the Falls Diner. He's a wonderful man." She seemed to gulp. "Are you staying on awhile in West Falls?"

He was feeling somewhat giddy about his impulsive decision. Although he'd wanted Holly to be the first one to hear about his plans, he couldn't resist the impulse to share the news with her closest friend.

"I made plans to stay in West Falls indefinitely. I signed a four-month lease with Doc, and I'm hoping to find some ranch work in the area. I've had a lot of experience breaking in wild horses and doctoring cattle back in Oklahoma."

Her eyes widened. "That can be dangerous."

"I served time in Afghanistan. There's nothing more life threatening than a combat zone."

He couldn't help but smile at her wide-eyed concern. Working with wild horses was something he'd been doing since his teen years, ever since his father had hired him on as a ranch hand at the Bar M Ranch. Every year during summer vacation he'd lived and worked at the Bar M, devoting himself to the business of cattle ranching. The whole reason he'd signed on at first was to repair his fractured relationship with his father. It had hurt his mother terribly to see him working side by side with the man who never publicly claimed him. *Crumbs,* she'd called it. "He's giving you nothing but crumbs," she'd said with tears misting in her eyes. "You deserve so much better." In the end, he'd learned the hard way that some fences could never be mended. It was the best lesson his father had ever taught him.

Yes indeed, working with wild horses could be dicey, but ranching had been in his blood for generations, even though for many years he'd resisted its strong pull. For years he'd asked himself why it appealed to him, and despite his many attempts to figure it all out, all he knew was that it called to him like an irresistible force. It wasn't a choice, he'd come to realize. It was his calling. And someday, he hoped to own his own spread, a little stretch of land he could call his own.

Dragging himself out of his thoughts, Dylan nodded, acknowledging her question. "Yeah, it can be dangerous. When horses are out of control, it can be an unstable situation. That's why training is so important."

She leaned forward in her chair. "And you've had lots of training, right?" She furrowed her brow, concern etched on her face.

He smiled, tickled by her earnestness. "Yeah, lots and lots. But I'm also very careful, and I respect the horses."

It was funny. She seemed to heave a huge sigh of relief. Cassidy was a sweetheart, that was for sure. Her caring so much about a perfect stranger showed she was a loving and giving woman. Again, he found himself wondering what had happened to devastate this young woman's life.

He quickly glanced at his watch. "Well, I should be heading back into town, since it looks like she won't be here for a while. It was nice meeting you, Cassidy."

She mumbled a goodbye. He heard the door close behind him and the turn of the lock as soon as he'd stepped out onto the porch. He stopped in his tracks as a feeling of unease came over him. He didn't know if he was being paranoid, but her actions had been a little strange. Although she seemed to radiate a good vibe, she'd been jumpy and nervous the entire time, even locking the door upon his departure. As he made his way to his car, he looked across the huge expanse of land that stretched out before him for miles and miles. Horseshoe Bend Ranch. He couldn't imagine a more tranquil place to live. It didn't seem the type of place where one had to bolt the door against intruders. What did he know about it anyway? Joy pulsed inside him as the realization hit him full force. He and Holly were now in the same zip code, and it wouldn't be much longer until they could see each other.

Had she really just done that? Rather than come clean with Dylan, she'd introduced herself to him as Cassidy Blake, the name of her best friend. She watched from behind a living room curtain as Dylan made his way off the front porch. He was handsome. That was for sure. Way more good-looking than his pictures captured. Those green eyes of his sparkled and glittered like a flawless gem. He had a beautiful, pearly-white grin. His dark hair was cut into a short military style, which enhanced his masculine features. And he was tall, six feet she would guess, with brawny arms and shoulders. His physicality was hard to ignore. It jumped out at her, reminding her of everything that set them apart from one another. Several times she'd wanted to reach out and grab his hand or ask him about Leo, his bearded dragon. But that would have been a huge tip-off that she wasn't who she was claiming to be. She'd sunk so low in hiding her disability from Dylan. Why hadn't she just told him? Surely it would have been better than these feelings of dread and guilt gnawing at her conscience. Pain sliced through her, causing her to wrap her arms around her middle in an attempt to assuage the hurt she'd inflicted on herself.

Lord, please make this pain go away. I've gotten so used to loss that I never knew it would hurt this much to lose Dylan before I truly had him. I try so hard to walk a righteous path, yet here I am withholding information and pretending to be somebody I'm not.

Was it really so out of the question to admit the truth to him? She squeezed her eyes shut to block out random images flashing into her mind. Dylan's shocked face as she introduced herself as the woman he'd been writing to over the past year. Dylan's disappointed expression. The look of pity that would inevitably pass over his face.

She covered her face with her hands. No, she couldn't do it. She couldn't handle the pain that came with the knowledge that she would never be Dylan's vision of what a partner should be. She was too flawed, too imperfect. He'd traveled all this way to see in person the woman he'd connected with during some of the darkest hours of his life. Never in a million years would Dylan be expecting a woman in a wheelchair. After all he'd been through in Afghanistan, she couldn't deliver him yet another blow. She just couldn't handle it.

As soon as she saw Dylan's truck zoom off into the distance, she picked up her cell phone and dialed the number of Cassidy Blake's art gallery. After a few rings, she heard her best friend's chirpy voice on the other end.

"Hi, Holly. What's up?"

"Cassidy. I need you to come to the ranch as quick

as you can get here." She felt out of breath after she finished.

"What is it? Are you okay?" Cassidy asked. Holly could hear the concern in her voice.

"It's not an emergency. I just need my best friend," she explained, trying to convey the urgency without causing Cassidy panic.

"Let me close up the gallery. I'll be there in twenty minutes," Cassidy promised, quickly ending the phone call.

For the next twenty minutes Holly fretted over her situation, wondering how she was going to tell Cassidy she'd impersonated her when Dylan had arrived at the ranch. Hopefully her best friend would understand the impossible position she was in. As soon as Holly heard the crunch of tires in the driveway, she made her way toward the door, opening it and greeting Cassidy as she quickly walked up the front steps.

As usual, her best friend radiated an effortless, breezy look. With her strawberry-blond hair, green eyes and wholesome good looks, she'd always been a show-stopper. Even in her simple T-shirt and flouncy skirt, she looked amazing.

Holly couldn't be happier about Cassidy's engagement to her older brother, Tate. They'd all been through a lot together, most notably the terrible accident that had left Holly without the use of her legs. For many years Cassidy had stayed away from West Falls, torn apart by guilt and shame since she had been behind the wheel at the time of the accident. Last summer Cassidy had returned home to help her ailing mother, and in the process, she and Tate had fallen in love all over again.

"You scared me with that phone call. What's going on?" Cassidy asked as she stepped over the threshold. She held out Dylan's letter to Holly. "You must have dropped this. I found it next to the mailbox."

Holly pushed the door closed and wheeled around so she could face Cassidy. She reached for the letter, stuffing it down into her skirt pocket. She took a deep breath.

"Do you remember me telling you about Dylan? The soldier I write to?"

"Of course. He's stationed in Afghanistan, right?"

Holly nodded. "Yes, he was. But he's stateside now. He arrived in West Falls today."

"That's amazing!" Cassidy squealed. "I can't wait to meet him."

Holly stared blankly at her best friend. In her opinion there was absolutely nothing to celebrate, although Cassidy had no way of knowing it.

Cassidy frowned, her eyes filled with concern. "What's the matter? You look as if someone died. I thought you'd be celebrating instead of moping around the house."

Holly looked down, too overcome with shame to look Cassidy in the eye. "Cass, I messed up. I didn't tell him about my being a paraplegic."

Cassidy's eyes bulged, and she shook her head in disbelief. After a few seconds she said, "Tell me everything."

Holly quickly got Cassidy up to speed on Dylan's unexpected visit and her pretense about being Cassidy.

"But how could you pretend to be me? We don't look anything alike. I thought you two sent pictures back and forth," Cassidy asked, her brow furrowed in confusion.

"I kept meaning to send a photo, but I never did. It was difficult to send him a picture without having told him I'm a paraplegic." Holly let out a bitter laugh. "Of course, when he showed up here he wasn't expecting to see his pen pal confined to a wheelchair, since I conveniently left that part out."

Cassidy looked agitated. She bit her lip and ran her fingers through her long hair. "What are you going to do?"

Holly was wringing her hands. She looked up at Cassidy, squashing down the spark of jealousy she felt as she gazed at her beautiful and able-bodied friend. Cassidy's calves were shapely, while hers lacked any muscle tone whatsoever. What she wouldn't give to be able to walk into a room under her own steam instead of always making an entrance by way of her wheelchair. She let out a deep sigh. What was the point of comparing herself to her best friend? She chided herself. Feeling envy wasn't going to change a thing. It wouldn't make her something she wasn't or somebody she could never be.

"I need you to pretend to be me, Cass. Just long enough so you can end things with him and send him on his way. He'll never know that you're not me." The words tumbled out of Holly's mouth at a rapid speed. Intuition told her that it was only a matter of time before Dylan came back to the ranch. He'd had a look of determination and purpose in his eyes. She needed to fix things quickly. Cassidy frowned. "Holly. You can't be serious. Why in the world would you want me to pretend to be you?"

Tears pricked her eyes. "I need you to do this for

me, Cass. Seriously. I want Dylan to leave West Falls and go back home to Oklahoma. This is the only way!" She was starting to feel desperate, as if the walls were closing in on her.

Cassidy frowned. "Tricking him isn't the answer. Why can't you just tell him the truth?"

Heat seared her cheeks. "Because I can't face him. I never told him I'm in a wheelchair, that I'm paralyzed from the waist down. How do you think he's going to feel after coming all this way to see me?"

"You're the bravest person I know. Find your words and tell him the truth. If he's as wonderful as you say he is, he'll understand."

"This is different. Dylan is... He's everything. Smart. Brave. Gorgeous."

Cassidy's brow was furrowed. "And you're all those things, Holly."

Holly shook her head. "No, I'm not, Cass. You don't understand. He's a soldier. The world he lives in is a very physical world. He breaks in wild horses, rides mountain bikes, does marathons. He protects America from harm. He's a hero."

"And you're pretty heroic, too. You've lived through a horrific accident that cost you the use of your legs. You've devoted your life to getting the message out about irresponsible teen driving. You're a woman of faith, Holly. All those things make you an amazing woman."

Although she loved Cassidy like a sister, she didn't want to hear any of this at the moment. It didn't matter how many times people told her she was brave and wonderful. She didn't feel either of those things. Not at the moment. Not when Dylan was most likely on his way back to the ranch to meet up with her. There was no way she could look him in the eye and admit her lies. She needed to get herself straightened out before he showed up.

"Please, Cassidy. I need you to be me when Dylan comes back," she begged in a panicked voice. "You owe me."

The ominous words hung in the air between them. Cassidy's face lost all of its color, and her mouth tightened in a firm line. As soon as the words had tumbled out of her mouth, Holly had deeply regretted them. Cassidy had just come back into her life after an eight-year absence. In the past six months they'd rebuilt a friendship that had been ruined in the aftermath of the accident that had left Holly paralyzed. Cassidy had been at the wheel at the time, and she'd fled West Falls rather than face the town's censure. It had taken a lot of hard work and prayer to get things back to where they once were with their friendship.

Now, due to overwhelming fear, Holly found herself in an awkward position. With three thoughtless words she'd dredged up their painful past and made Cassidy feel as if she were still harboring a grudge. In reality she, along with Cassidy's cousin, Regina Blake, and their childhood friend, Jenna Keegan, all shared in the responsibility. They'd all participated in the reckless-driving game, although Cassidy had taken the fall since she'd been at the wheel when the car had slid off the road. One could make the argument that she, in fact, owed Cassidy everything for having single-handedly shouldered the blame for eight long years.

Before she could apologize, a knock sounded at the

door. Holly jerked her head in the direction of the front door, then looked over at Cassidy. Her friend's eyes were wide with alarm, and she was shaking her head back and forth.

"Please, Cassidy. Just pretend to be me. Tell him you started seeing someone, that you're really sorry but it's over," Holly whispered. She felt weak begging Cassidy to do something she knew was wrong, but a part of her didn't care. Right now all she cared about was making sure Dylan didn't figure out his pen pal was confined to a wheelchair.

"Tell the truth, Holly. Before this whole thing spirals out of control," Cassidy said, her eyes full of disappointment.

Feeling defiant, Holly wheeled over to the door and yanked it open. All of the air rushed out of her lungs the moment she saw Dylan. He was wearing a black cowboy hat, but he quickly took it off and placed it by his side. She noticed he'd switched up his clothes and taken a shower. His hair was still slightly damp, and he was wearing a pair of jeans and a white T-shirt. His arms were heavily muscled and toned. Once again, she was hit with the full impact of Dylan's physicality. He looked as if he belonged on the cover of a men's fitness magazine or on television as the star of a healthy-living commercial. All at once it hit her smack on the head. There was no way she belonged in his world. For the past year she'd been living in a world of denial, clinging to a kernel of hope about a possible future with this impossibly perfect man. In his arms was a bouquet of yellow roses and white stargazer lilies, her favorite flowers. Somehow he'd remembered from her letters.

She felt a pang run through her at his thoughtfulness. How she wanted to reach out and accept his offering and press her nose against the fragrant blooms.

"Is she back yet?" Dylan asked, his expressive eyes radiating enthusiasm.

With a lump in her throat, all she could do was nod and gesture toward the inside of the house. His handsome face lit up with a wide grin. She smiled at him, feeling light-headed at the sight of his tall, muscular frame. But he wasn't smiling at her. He was looking past her, straight at Cassidy. And he was beaming so widely it almost overtook his whole face. She felt her chest tighten painfully. Loss—sharp and swift—flooded her. How could it be this painful to lose something she'd never truly had in the first place? Sucking in a ragged breath, she invited him inside, then watched as he walked across the threshold and beat a fast path toward her best friend.

Chapter Two

"Holly! Is it you?" Dylan made his way across the foyer in two quick strides. Cassidy nodded her head in acknowledgment. Holly watched as Dylan wrapped his arms around Cassidy in a warm embrace. She felt her insides lurch as she observed Dylan's intimate gesture. He was so full of life, so enthusiastic and joyful. Watching him was like seeing a force of nature in motion. Her best friend, on the other hand, was acting standoffish. She wasn't hugging Dylan back, and her body language was as stiff as a board. Her expressive face was giving away too much. Maybe it was simply because she knew her so well that she could tell Cassidy looked conflicted and ill at ease. Her pulse started beating at a rapid pace. If Cassidy couldn't pull this off, she'd be forced to explain it all to Dylan. The very thought of it made her palms sweat.

A part of her couldn't help but feel cheated as she watched Dylan's interaction with her best friend. This embrace should have been hers. His gorgeous smile, which lit the room up like sunshine, should have been directed at her. And maybe it would have been, she thought. If only she had been honest with him from the beginning. Perhaps things could have been different.

Cassidy stepped away from the hug, her face paler than usual, her eyes drifting nervously away from Dylan and toward Holly. She seemed as if she was in pain. Guilt speared through her at the agony on her best friend's face. She looked as if she'd rather go swimming with sharks than follow through with this meeting.

"This has been a long time coming." Dylan's voice was infused with sweetness. To Holly it sounded like the sweet sound of rain after a long drought. For a moment she let it wash over her, rejoicing in the rich timbre of it. He held out the bouquet of flowers, saying, "These are for you," as he handed them over.

"Thank you. They're gorgeous," Cassidy said stiffly, reaching out and accepting the stunning flowers.

Dylan grinned, showcasing a pair of dazzling dimples. "I hope you're not upset with me for showing up here in West Falls. I'm not usually a fly-by-the-seat-of-my-pants guy, but I couldn't help myself. The way you described your hometown made me want to see it for myself."

"It's definitely unexpected," Cassidy answered, shooting Holly a meaningful look.

Holly tried to nod discreetly in Cassidy's direction, wanting to encourage her to act normal, but she felt Dylan's gaze land on her. He seemed to have the instincts of a hawk, paying close attention to everything around him. As a soldier, he'd probably honed those skills as a means of survival.

Dylan frowned. "Did I interrupt y'all in the middle of something?"

"No, of course not," Holly said smoothly, her eyes now focused on Dylan's face.

"It's fine. We were just shooting the breeze," Cassidy added. "Would you like something to drink? Some sweet tea or lemonade?"

"I'd love some sweet tea," he answered, looking grateful for the offer.

"Sure thing. It'll give me a chance to put these flowers in a vase." Cassidy scurried off toward the kitchen, as if she couldn't wait to escape, leaving the two of them all by themselves.

"Why don't you make yourself comfortable in the living room." Holly gestured toward the doorway leading to the foyer. Following behind him, she quickly maneuvered her wheelchair into the room. As Dylan folded his tall, rugged body into a leather armchair, her gaze was drawn to the dog tags hanging around his neck.

Filled with curiosity, she blurted, "Are those your tags?"

Dylan reached up and lightly fingered the tags, his face contemplative as he answered. "Just one of 'em is mine. The other one belonged to one of my buddies who died over in Afghanistan."

Died? He must be referring to Benji, the soldier he'd written about in one of his letters. At only eighteen years old, he'd been among the youngest soldiers in the unit. From what she remembered, he'd been killed instantly when their Humvee had been blown up by a roadside bomb. Dylan had been seriously injured as well, but thankfully had rebounded from those injuries. The attack had occurred before they'd started writing each other, and Dylan was very close lipped about it and his subsequent hospitalization and recovery.

Cassidy returned with a tray of drinks and some slices of homemade pumpkin bread. Like a perfect hostess, she served the refreshments, then plopped down onto the sofa directly across from Dylan. Holly discreetly watched him as he thirstily downed the contents of the glass. It was almost impossible to tear her gaze away from him. She felt like a starving person sitting down at an all-you-can-eat buffet. Dylan, in all his cowboy/soldier glory was a sight for sore eyes.

"Horseshoe Bend Ranch is spectacular," he raved, his eyes wide with admiration. "I can't say as I've ever seen a finer spread." His tone was filled with awe.

"It's the largest and most profitable horse-and-cattle-breeding operation in this part of the state." The words rolled off Holly's tongue like quicksilver. She wanted to clap her hands over her mouth to stop herself from inserting herself into the conversation. It wasn't her place to crow about the family ranch. That might raise a red flag in Dylan's eyes.

Dylan grinned at her. "I'm not at all surprised to hear that." He turned his gaze toward Cassidy. "It must make you feel proud knowing what your family has achieved."

"Yes, the Lynches are a hardworking bunch," Cassidy acknowledged. "It's impossible not to feel proud of them."

Holly flashed a smile in her soon-to-be sister-in-law's direction. Her best friend was incredibly sweet and loyal. As far as she was concerned, Cassidy was going to be a perfect addition to the Lynch clan. If Cassidy and Tate would only set a date and put everyone out of their misery!

"So I was thinking you might like to grab a bite to eat in town," Dylan said, his face full of expectation. "It'll give us a chance to talk for a spell."

White teeth flashed against his sun-burnished skin, causing a little hitch in her heart at the beauty of his smile.

Cassidy pressed her fingertips against her head. "Dylan, I—I'm not feeling too well." She shifted uncomfortably in her seat. "I'm so happy you stopped by, but I think it might be better if we catch up another time."

Dylan's face fell. He recovered quickly, plastering a smile on his face. "Sure thing. Why don't I swing by tomorrow. I think I'll head back to town and grab something to eat. Doc tells me I have a standing invitation at his diner."

Dylan stood up, placing his empty glass down on the tray before reaching for his Stetson and resting it against his chest.

The look on Dylan's face took her breath away. He looked confused. And crushed. Some of the light went out of his eyes. Holly wanted to wrap her arms around him and soothe his disappointment. Although he appeared to be as tough as nails on the outside, with his rugged appearance and soldier's swagger, she knew all too well about his tender side. And even though she felt a twinge of annoyance toward Cassidy for going off script, she knew all the blame for this entire fiasco lay at her feet. She'd done this. Her insecurities about believing a man could fall for her had led her down this path. For more than twelve months she'd neglected to tell him her most basic truth. And now it was all unraveling, bit by bit.

Of course, it had all begun innocently enough. Pastor Blake had started a pen-pal program so the members of Main Street Church could correspond with soldiers serving in Afghanistan. Wanting to show her support for the brave men and women of the armed forces, she'd quickly signed up. From the very beginning she'd felt a connection with the brave soldier from Madden, Oklahoma. They'd shared their hopes and dreams, as well as favorite movies, stories about their pets and bestloved ice cream flavors. She'd shared tidbits with him about life in West Falls and the joys of Horseshoe Bend Ranch, as well as her loving family.

In turn, he'd described a soldier's day-to-day life in Afghanistan, the triumphs, the tragedies and the struggles. He'd written her about his wonderful mother, who'd raised him as a single parent. One letter led to another until they were receiving letters from each other on a weekly basis. Somehow, without her even realizing it, Dylan Hart had become a huge part of her life. As the door closed behind Dylan, a feeling of emptiness swept through her like a strong gust of wind. A longing to call out to him, to stop him in his tracks so she could make him stay longer, rose up inside her. After so many nights lying awake, thinking about her green-eyed soldier, it was agonizing knowing she would never be able to face him as Holly Lynch. As much as she wished it wasn't true, Dylan Hart would forever be out of her reach.

* * *

Dylan didn't know how to explain the feelings roaring through him as he headed out the gates of Horseshoe Bend Ranch. He felt like a deflated balloon. For the life of him, he couldn't figure out why he felt so disappointed. Holly was gorgeous. Stunning. Any normal, red-blooded man would take one look at her and thank the Lord above for placing her in his orbit. But when he'd finally come face-to-face with her, there had been no kismet, no spark. Nothing special. She hadn't even seemed stoked to see him.

Could he have been so wrong about their connection? She'd been much quieter than he'd ever imagined. In her letters, her lively personality had practically jumped off the page. In person, Holly hadn't been at all as he'd imagined. Something felt off between them. There hadn't been a feeling of recognition when he met her. Not at all. Not even for a single minute. Although he knew it would take some time for them to adjust to each other, things still should have flowed more effortlessly between them. There had been no attraction, no pull in her direction. And she wasn't at all like he'd expected her to be. She was skittish and nervous. When he'd moved to pull her into a hug, she'd stood there like a statue, still and unmoving. She hadn't even hugged him back. She didn't seem like the Holly he'd gotten to know over the past twelve months.

And then she'd practically rushed him out the door on the pretext of not feeling well. Not once had she asked about his living arrangements or his four-month rental with Doc Sampson. Truthfully, she hadn't seemed all that happy to see him at Horseshoe Bend Ranch.

Disappointment filled him, leaving him frustrated and full of sorrow. He'd been so sure about Holly, more certain of her than anything ever in his life. Yet now it was looking as if he'd made another gigantic mistake.

It wouldn't be the first time, a little voice reminded him. He shook off the memory of his faithless ex-girlfriend, Shawna. It had been a long time since he'd thought about his high school sweetheart, the woman who'd dumped him after his deployment to Afghanistan. After he'd broken his neck and was laid up in a military hospital, he'd been deemed useless in her eyes. He fought against the anger swelling up inside him. There was no time in his life for people who weren't genuine. And he refused to wallow over past hurts. He had enough scars to last a lifetime.

Please don't let me have been so mistaken about Holly. I've been so wrong in the past about so many things—relationships, people, situations. Please let me find in her the strong, faithful woman I've been seeking. Show me I haven't traveled all this way chasing a pipe dream.

Maybe it was just jitters from meeting each other for the first time. It could be that his expectations were way too high. And meeting someone in the flesh was a lot different than writing to one another. She had every right to be nervous, didn't she? Perhaps it just wasn't meant to be, he realized as a sinking sensation settled in his stomach. Being so misguided about a situation would be a hard pill to swallow. Sometimes one just got a sense of a person—who they were down to their very soul. And for the past year, he'd come to know Holly as a warm and loving, God-fearing woman. Her goodness had resonated in every letter she'd written him and wormed its way inside him, serving as a reminder of everything he wanted in a life partner.

Try as he might, he just couldn't shake off the encounter with Holly. There was something bothering him. It was resting right under the surface, but he couldn't put his finger on it. All of a sudden it hit him. Her eyes. They'd been a vivid green, not blue. Holly had said her eyes were blue. Or was he going crazy? And he'd noticed she was wearing a ring when she'd poured him the sweet tea. Not just any ring, he realized. It had been a diamond ring planted on the wedding finger of her left hand.

He pulled his truck over to the side of the road, his breathing shallow as he racked his brain for the facts. Had she been wearing an engagement ring? Could he have been wrong about her eye color? No, absolutely not. He remembered the words she'd written him in her letter. *I'm a blue-eyed girl from West Falls, Texas.*

He slammed his palm against the steering wheel. What in the world was going on? The woman he'd just seen, the one pretending to be Holly, was a fraud. Her eyes were a spectacular green. That fact, coupled with the odd way she'd been acting and the sparkly ring, was all the proof he needed. With a wild groan, he did a U-turn in the road, his tires spewing dust and rocks as he made his way back toward Horseshoe Bend Ranch. He didn't know who was trying to make a fool out of him, but he was surely going to find out.

"That did not go so well." Holly let out a deep sigh. Things had not unfolded the way she'd envisioned. Even though she hated the idea of tricking Dylan, the idea had come to her in a moment of absolute desperation. As an honest woman, it didn't sit well with her that she'd taken the low road instead of coming clean to Dylan. An overwhelming feeling of fear had held her back. She now felt as helpless as a lamb.

"Holly, I'm sorry. I tried, but I—" Cassidy grimaced and shook her head. "I just couldn't pull it off the way you wanted. It didn't feel right giving him the brush-off."

"It's not your fault. I'm responsible." Her tone was clipped. She saw the look of dismay on her best friend's face. She didn't mean to be so abrupt, but she was feeling so wounded. It hurt to lose the possibility of Dylan. Even though they'd shared secrets and dreams ever since they were kids, she wanted to lick her wounds in private. There was no way Cassidy could ever understand what had driven her to keep her disability a secret. Most able-bodied people wouldn't get it in a million years. All Cassidy had to do was walk in a room to have all male eyes drawn to her like moths to a flame. Ever since the accident she'd been single. Alone. For eight long years she hadn't gone out on a date or shared a sweet, tender kiss with a single soul. There had been nobody to hold hands with or catch a movie with at the drive-in. She'd hadn't received flowers on Valentine's Day or kissed anyone under the mistletoe. Although she'd felt the stirrings of something with Deputy Cullen Brand, they'd never managed to get out of the friend zone. And considering the fact that he worked closely with Tate in the sheriff's office, in the long run it might have been a little awkward.

Becoming Dylan's correspondent had allowed her a rare opportunity to connect with someone without her physical condition being front and center. Living in a small town like West Falls where everyone knew her whole life story felt limiting at times. And she'd wanted to experience romance. Pure, wondrous romance.

She'd wanted someone to fall for her without the wheelchair getting in the way. Yes, in retrospect it was selfish of her to withhold the truth, but she hadn't been able to write those words down on the page. She hadn't wanted his opinion of her to change.

Her relationship with Dylan had started out as mere friendship, blossoming into tender, powerful feelings over the course of the past year. Deep in her soul she'd nurtured a fragile hope that he might be the one. She'd never been in love, but she'd hoped to be in a position to fall head over heels in love with Dylan. And to have those tender feelings returned. Now, in light of everything, those dreams had gone up in smoke. She must have been crazy to think this would all work out in the end.

The sound of whirring tires followed by screeching brakes reverberated in the stillness of the October afternoon. A loud rapping on the front door soon followed. Holly locked eyes with Cassidy before moving toward the front door and slowly opening it. Dylan was standing on the front porch, his handsome features marred by a frown. Holly let out a deep breath. He looked so different now. His face was shuttered. He seemed impenetrable, as if he'd built a wall around himself no one or nothing could breach. The way he was standing—his arms were folded in front of him and his chest was rapidly rising and falling—caused a prickle of awareness to race through her. He looked as if he were ready to take on the world.

"May I come in?" The grim set of his features was nothing compared to the iciness in his voice.

Flustered, Holly waved him into the house. All the while her mind was racing. What was he doing back here? And why was his expression so forbidding? Her throat felt constricted, and she didn't think she could utter a single word if she tried. The sound of his boots echoed sharply against the hardwood floor. He moved toward the middle of the foyer so he was facing both of them.

Looking back and forth between them, he ground out, "Make no mistake, we need to get something straight. I don't know what kind of game the two of you are playing with me, but I do know you're not Holly Lynch." He jutted his chin in Cassidy's direction, his eyes blazing with anger. "Are you?"

Resembling a deer caught in headlights, Cassidy froze, her eyes wide with alarm.

Holly maneuvered her wheelchair until she was positioned directly in front of Cassidy. She had no intention of making her best friend take it on the chin. She'd started this whole thing, and even though it wouldn't be easy, facing Dylan was her responsibility. She looked up at him, refusing to lose her courage and look away from his probing gaze.

Before losing her nerve, she dived right in. "You're right. She's not Holly, Dylan. I am."

Chapter Three

"Holly?" His question bristled in the air like a live grenade. The air around them buzzed with electricity.

"Yes. It's me, Dylan." She met his gaze head on, her blue eyes full of intensity.

A hundred different thoughts were swirling through his mind. His first reaction was a strong sense of recognition. Of course this was Holly. It all made sense now, and even though he'd been thrown off by the wheelchair, there was something he'd instantly recognized in her essence.

His second reaction was sorrow. His soul shattered for Holly. *She couldn't walk?* The same woman he'd been corresponding with for more than a solid year was in a wheelchair. Hadn't she written him about being an accomplished rider? About wanting a house full of kids one day? What had happened to her? Had this all been a big scam? Thoughts were whizzing through his brain until he felt himself becoming dizzy.

Confusion covered him like a shroud. His mind went

totally blank. Suddenly, he was stumbling around in the darkness without a way out.

"Why?" His voice came out raspy and uneven. He shoved his fingers through his hair as myriad emotions flitted through him. "Why didn't you tell me? What is this all about?" The tone of his voice sounded sharp and raised, but he was well past caring about that. It hurt so badly that Holly had tried to trick him. The chocolate Labrador retriever began growling low in his throat, the hairs on his back raised. The dog sat down in front of Holly, acting as a protector.

"Shush, Bingo. Quiet down," Holly said in a firm voice as she patted the top of his head.

Cassidy cleared her throat and looked over at Holly, her eyes wide with concern. "Holly. What do you want me to do? Should I stay?"

Holly met Cassidy's gaze. She gave her best friend a tentative smile and shook her head. "Go back to the gallery, Cass. I'm sorry I involved you in this."

Cassidy glanced back and forth between them, hesitating for a moment before she headed for the door. She pulled it open and cast a lingering glance over her shoulder at the two of them. The look in her eyes warned him to go easy on Holly. The sound of the door clicking closed behind her rang out in the stillness of the foyer.

The silence that lingered in Cassidy's wake was painful. Considering written communication between them had always felt effortless, it was an odd sensation.

"I'm sorry, Dylan. Please don't blame Cassidy for pretending to be me. It was all my idea. And it's not something I'm proud of by any means."

"Then why'd you do it?" he asked, needing to know what this ruse was all about.

"When I got your letter today, I panicked," she admitted. She gestured toward her legs. "Not telling you about my being paralyzed was cowardly. I should have told you in the very beginning, but as time went by, it became harder and harder." She hung her head. "I should never have kept secrets from you, Dylan. It was wrong of me."

"When? How?" He was fumbling with his words. There was so much he wanted to say, to ask, but he still felt out of sorts. He was still reeling from the news. The shock reverberated down to his very core.

"I was in a car accident when I was eighteen, right after I graduated from high school. My friends and I were playing a reckless-driving game, and I didn't have my seat belt on. The roads were slick that night, and we weren't being responsible. Cassidy lost control and hit a stone wall. I was thrown from the car." Holly's shoulders sagged. "As a result, I lost the use of my legs."

His mouth felt as dry as sandpaper. He had to ask the question, couldn't deal with not knowing. Already it was nagging at him relentlessly.

"Permanently?" His voice sounded like a croak.

"Yes. My spinal cord was partially severed. Even though I still have some sensation, I won't ever walk again. Not in this lifetime."

The words slammed into him with the force of a tidal wave. The news left him feeling unsteady on his feet. It felt like a kick in the gut. He felt so selfish for thinking it, but there it was, settled firmly around his heart. Why hadn't she told him? His hands were trembling like a leaf. He felt such incredible disappointment in her decision to withhold something so important from him. As a person who'd been caught in a web of lies ever since he was born, he was a big believer in the truth. And Holly had seemed so open and forthright in her letters. Had he been mistaken? Everything he'd dreamed of building with Holly had crashed and burned in a single instant. And he felt nauseous. Sick with loss and grief and dashed hopes. And he also felt devastated for her. Sweet, loyal Holly, who'd written to him over weeks and months without fail. She'd sent him care packages filled with treats and books and stuffed animals. Holly had kept him in her prayers, and in return, he'd asked God to keep her out of harm's way. Wonderful, brave Holly, who'd no doubt been through so much pain and tragedy in her young life. Yet in her letters she'd always projected such positivity, like a strong ray of sunshine beaming down on him in a war-torn, unstable land.

Still, it didn't sit well with him that she hadn't come clean to him. It made him question every single thing he knew about her. He'd traveled all this way to meet her, all in the hopes of starting a life with her. In his mind, he'd begun to think of her in a forever type of way. The ring, the white picket fence, the kids, promises of forever. Once again, he'd been a prize fool. *Counting chickens,* his mother called it, and she'd been warning him against doing so ever since he was knee high to a grasshopper.

And there was something else. Holly being in a wheelchair brought him back to a place and time where he himself had been disabled. A roadside bomb in Afghanistan had blown the Humvee he was driving to smithereens. Two soldiers in his unit had been killed, with another losing his sight. The injuries he'd sustained due to the IED had been life threatening. In the beginning, he'd been told he might never walk again. But, over weeks and months he'd crawled his way out of the dark, black hole and gotten his life back. And to prove a point, he'd volunteered for another tour, just to show he hadn't been beaten. He was still standing.

"I'm sorry you came all the way here only to be disappointed."

Holly's melodic voice dragged him out of the past, so that his feet were solidly planted in the here and now. And even though he wanted to run from this situation, he had no choice but to face it. "No, it's not about that. It's just—" Just what? How could he explain it to Holly without hurting her or making her feel more ashamed of the information she'd withheld? He needed to be sensitive to her feelings, but at the same time, he couldn't sugarcoat things. He had to be honest with himself as well as Holly. So far, things were not playing out as he'd imagined.

"I suppose you had a preconceived notion about me, right? Cute. Blond. Blue-eyed. Standing on two feet." She breathed out a tiny huff of air. "Wheelchairs don't exactly come to mind when you're painting a picture in your head of someone, do they?"

He let out a ragged sigh, then raked his fingers through his military cut. "I don't know what to say, what to think." He rocked back on his boots, then looked away from her intense scrutiny. She seemed to be studying him, and it made him feel slightly uncomfortable. With a groan he turned back toward her. "I'm being honest here. If I'd known from the beginning, I'm sure I wouldn't be feeling this way." He shook his head, trying to rid his mind of all the jumbled thoughts. "Okay, that's not true. Or maybe it is. I don't know how I would feel, Holly. I just feel a little caught off guard. You weren't straight with me. Don't you think I deserved to know? It makes me wonder if you were ever planning to come clean with me." Although it pained him a little to press the point, he felt he deserved an explanation.

Holly nodded, and he saw a soft sheen glimmering in her eyes. Those incredible blue eyes he'd been dreaming about gazing into were awash in tears. For the first time he noticed how pretty she was, and if it hadn't been for the wheelchair, he might have recognized her right off. It had thrown him, since he'd never been given a single hint about her condition. And he hated to admit it, but he'd looked right through her. The wheelchair had served as a barrier to the truth.

He'd been under the belief that there wasn't a single thing about Holly he didn't know. She was his champion. His Texas rose. The woman he'd been so wrapped up in for the past twelve months. But when she'd greeted him at the door, the wheelchair had served as a buffer between them, and it made him feel a little small to realize that he hadn't even really given her more than a cursory glance.

"Of course you had a right to know, especially when we started discussing the future and meeting one another in person. And I did plan to meet you...on my own terms, when I was ready to tell you everything." Tears slid down her face. Her chin trembled and quivered. Despite it all, she held her head up high. Her countenance said a lot about her. She was strong. She'd had to be, he reckoned. Being paralyzed at the tender age of eighteen didn't leave one a lot of choices, did it? He had a hunch Holly had dug in deep and persevered, relying on her faith and family to sustain her.

"Believe it or not, I'm pretty courageous in most other aspects of my life. For some reason, I just didn't have the guts to tell you the truth. I kept promising myself I would with each and every letter, but as time moved on, it became more and more difficult to do so."

Suddenly, the tables had turned. Just like that, his anger fizzled. Instead of feeling upset with her, he was now feeling badly for Holly. It was confusing, since he was the one who'd been deceived. He was the one who had no idea where he went from here. With no job, four months of rent paid up to Doc Sampson and nothing going the way he'd imagined, his future was seriously in question. All he knew was that he wanted to comfort this woman he'd grown to care about.

"Hey, don't cry, Holly. My mama always told me a pretty girl should never cry." He got down on his haunches beside her chair, then leaned over and brushed her tears away with his thumb.

"At least you think I'm pretty," she joked, the corners of her mouth creasing in a slight smile. Her dry comment made him want to grin back at her, even though the circumstances didn't exactly call for it. Wheelchair or no wheelchair, she still had withheld vital information from him. She hadn't been half as transparent as she'd seemed on paper.

Holly was far more than pretty, he realized. Beautiful, even. He started to tell her so, but he stopped, determined not to go down that road. Not today when so many things were up in the air between them. Not when his stomach was tangled up in knots and he couldn't seem to think past this very moment. The intense feeling holding him in its grip was easily recognizable. It was fear. Because even though he was a decorated soldier who had served two tours of duty in Afghanistan, the thought of Holly being in a wheelchair sent anxiety racing through him.

And even though he still cared about her, he wasn't certain he saw a future for the two of them. Call it crazy, but ever since Holly had come into his life, dreams of them together forever filled his head at night as he drifted off to slumber. Although he felt a stab of guilt for even thinking it, he couldn't deny the doubts coursing through him. He'd just made it home from a combat zone after seeing his fellow soldiers and civilians broken and bloodied and lifeless. He wasn't sure he was up to any more challenges. Did knowing he might not be able to handle this make him a bad person?

Dear Lord, please give me some clarity. Holly is such a sweet, warm person, but I don't want to plunge headlong into a situation I can't emotionally handle. And I'm still really confused about where we go from here. A huge curveball was thrown at me when I wasn't expecting it. Life has shown me that everything happens for a reason, yet I can't fathom why I'm here. And I can't wrap my head around Holly being a paraplegic. It reminds me so much of everything I left behind in Afghanistan. Am I strong enough to get past this deception?

"What are you going to do now?" She looked at him

sorrowfully, her expression full of regret and a hundred different emotions he didn't want to analyze.

Dylan shrugged as reality set in. He really didn't have anyplace to go. With his mother having recently moved to New Mexico with her new husband, there was no longer anything tying him to his hometown. He'd burned all his bridges with his father a while ago, no longer content with being a dirty little secret. His outside child. The one who didn't matter. It had been almost six years since he'd spoken to him. He wasn't even certain his father knew he'd made it back from Afghanistan. Nor did he think he even cared. For too long now, he'd been seeking something from the man that he'd never been willing to give. Acceptance. Unconditional love.

At the moment he felt like a ship without a rudder. Here he was in West Falls, Texas, as clueless as the day he was born. For so long he'd been running. From his father. From the painful gibes about his paternity. He'd run away from Madden, Oklahoma, straight into the service. At some point he just had to stand still. And perhaps God had placed him here in West Falls for a reason.

He stroked his chin with his thumb, deep in thought. "My rent is paid up for the next four months, and I really don't have a lot of options. I need to find a job until I can get on my feet. From what I've seen, West Falls is a nice community."

Holly's eyes began to blink, and her mouth was agape. "You're staying?"

He was still filled with so much uncertainty, but this decision to stick around was based more on practical-

ity than anything else. In his current financial situation, losing several months' rent was a big deal. For
years he'd been sending the majority of his active-duty
paycheck back home to his mother. And even though
she'd socked some of it away for him in a bank account,
he was still far from being solvent. In order to realize his dreams of owning his own ranch, he needed to
keep making positive strides in that direction. Instead
of acting impulsively once again, he'd have to stick
around West Falls, at least until his lease ran out. And
perhaps he could find work to tide him over while he
was in town.

Holly's gaze was strong and steady. It made him
squirm some. Her eyes were such a deep, piercing blue.
They pulled him in, and for a moment, all he could do
was stare at her. Holly. His pen pal. His more than a
friend but not quite a girlfriend. At the moment she was
an enigma. As much as her letters had revealed about
her life at Horseshoe Bend Ranch, her family and her
abiding faith, she'd kept her disability a secret. Surely
there were ripple effects in her daily life because of the
accident and her being a paraplegic.

"Yep," he acknowledged begrudgingly. "It looks like
I'll be staying for a while."

Holly's eyes widened, and her throat convulsed as
she swallowed. "West Falls will welcome you with open
arms. And it would be fine with me if you wanted to
work here at the ranch. With your background, it would
make perfect sense."

Open arms? For some reason he couldn't imagine
it. His own hometown hadn't been half as accepting of
him and the single mother who'd raised him. No, they'd

been considered inferior due to his mother's unmarried status and the lack of a father figure in the picture. It hadn't helped matters that his mother had been stunningly beautiful, making all the married women in town clutch their husbands tightly to their sides whenever she was in their presence. She hadn't deserved their judgment and disapproval. Hurt roared through him as the bitter memories swept over him. There hadn't been an ounce of compassion or goodness in any of them!

Holly shot him a nervous smile. "It's a big place with plenty of work to keep you busy."

He nodded at her, his thoughts a jumbled mess. So far this day had not shaped up as he'd planned. And he had no one to blame but himself for much of it. "I'll think about it. It's mighty nice for you to suggest it," he said. "Especially since I showed up here out of the blue."

"I think it might work out nicely," she said, her expression a bit guarded. "If you're open to it."

He felt himself frowning. There was no way he was getting too optimistic about West Falls, even if the idea of a job at Horseshoe Bend Ranch seemed almost perfect. If he built up his hopes too high, he'd most likely be disappointed. He'd taken this huge leap of faith without thinking things through in a mature manner. And he'd gotten burned by her lie.

All this time he'd been focused on meeting Holly and building on the foundation they'd already established. But perhaps he'd really been doing what he'd always done. Running away. From Madden. From the fear of failure. From a father, who treated him like a castoff. Far away from gossipmongers and painful half-truths. Unknowingly, he'd run straight toward another complicated situation. He'd gotten involved with a woman who didn't think enough of him to be straight with him.

Although he'd been hopeful about finally finding peace in this town, things weren't half as simple as he'd envisioned. Just when he'd thought his life was about to be as calm as a lake in summer, a twist of fate had changed everything. At the moment he felt as uncertain about his future as when he'd been dodging land mines in the fields of Afghanistan.

"Picasso, you're a beauty," Holly cooed as she brushed the onyx-colored colt. With her other hand she reached up and fingered the white star on his forehead. She had a soft spot for the handsome horse who'd been born at Horseshoe Bend Ranch during a terrible storm last summer. Although the storm had greatly damaged Main Street Church, it had served as a catalyst to bring her brother and her best friend back together as a couple. For that she would always be grateful.

Rather than sitting at home fretting about the situation with Dylan, she'd gotten in her van and headed down the road to the stables. Being able to drive gave her a sense of independence. Once she was behind the wheel, the world didn't seem so small anymore. She didn't feel so much like a caged bird. And she was never more centered than when she was spending time with her horses. This was where she felt most comfortable, a place where her dreams resided.

One day, she vowed, she'd get back on a horse and ride across the beautiful landscape of Horseshoe Bend Ranch. Sadly, she'd never be able to ride in the same manner as she had before the car crash—wild, spirited galloping through the countryside. But she would still be able to experience the unforgettable sensation of being at one with her horses. For the first time in a long time, she'd be free.

Malachi, who'd worked at the ranch since she was a teenager, had given her space as soon as she'd gotten out of the van, seeming to know intuitively that she was seeking solitude the moment she'd shown up. With his dark, brooding eyes, prominent cheekbones and solemn expression, he was the strong, introspective type.

A few times he stepped outside the barn and checked on her, his movements stealthy as he watched her. It was almost enough to make her smile, watching Malachi observing her when he thought she wasn't paying attention.

Holly heard the crunch of tires on the dirt and the slam of a car door. Shuffling noises let her know someone was walking toward her. As the steps got closer and closer, she called out, "Uh-oh. I must be in trouble if the sheriff of West Falls is paying me a visit in the middle of the afternoon."

"What in the world is going on out here?" a male voice barked.

The sound of her brother's voice confirmed her hunch. She swiveled her head around and made eye contact with Tate, taking in his furrowed brow and the deep scowl on his face.

"Something tells me you already know." She knew Cassidy like the back of her hand. There was a time when she'd kept secrets from Tate—things that had almost doomed their relationship. Now that they were happily engaged, Cassidy wasn't going to hold back anything from the man she loved. She wouldn't do it, not even for her best friend. The stern look on her brother's face confirmed what she already suspected—Tate knew all about the circumstances surrounding Dylan's visit.

"Cassidy was quite upset. She told me the whole story. I had to practically pry it out of her to find out what you'd said to hurt her feelings so badly." Tate's mouth was pinched tightly, his brown eyes narrowed into slits. "Did you seriously throw the past in her face like that?"

Holly looked away and tucked her chin against her chest. She couldn't bear to see such disappointment in Tate's eyes. "I messed up. Big time. What I said to her about owing me—" Heat burned her cheeks as her own words came back to her.

"—should never have been said," Tate finished. His features were etched in grim lines.

Holly wiped her hand across her face, getting rid of the beads of sweat gathered on her forehead. "You have no idea how much I regret saying those words. I wouldn't hurt Cassidy for the world. You know that. I'm just not myself today. And I fully plan to meet up with her tomorrow and apologize."

Tate raised an eyebrow. His features softened. "Seems to me if it wasn't for this soldier friend of yours, you would never have gone to that hurtful place with Cassidy."

She fought against a rising sense of irritation with her brother. At twenty-six years old, she was responsible for her own actions. It was high time Tate stopped giving her a free pass.

"Please don't blame Dylan. None of this is his fault."

"So what exactly is he to you? A friend? Pen pal? Or something more?" Tate's voice was tinged with curiosity.

Holly sighed. Tate's question hit a sore spot. Although it was clear feelings had blossomed between the two of them over the course of more than a year, neither of them had ever laid their feelings on the line. And having a letter-writing relationship couldn't begin to compare to a real face-to-face interaction. Other than gut instinct, she didn't have any proof of Dylan's feelings. She had the feeling that coming to West Falls had been his way of exploring their relationship and showing her how much he wanted them to meet one-on-one. After all, hadn't Dylan written about wanting to say certain things to her in person? But now everything had changed. She'd been a fool to ever think she was on Dylan's level.

"We were building toward something. I'm pretty sure that's why he came all this way to see me." She let out a ragged breath, releasing the weight of the world from her shoulders. "For the first time since the accident, I felt as if I was developing a romantic rapport with someone. And I got carried away with those feelings. I can admit that. It felt so good to be treated like a whole person. I just didn't want that to end. That's why I hid the truth from him in all of my letters."

"Being a paraplegic doesn't make you any less of a person." Tate made a clucking sound. "The sight of you in a wheelchair shouldn't send him running."

"He has every right to be mad. And upset. And disappointed." She lowered her head, unable to look her brother in the eye.

Tate reached down and lifted up her chin. "Don't even go down that road. You could never be a disappointment. You're beautiful and funny and smart, with a heart as big as the outdoors."

"He doesn't see a future with me." The words clogged in her throat, and she fought the sudden urge to cry. Where had all her strength gone? Why did her insides feel like mush?

Tate scowled, looking every inch the tough Texas lawman. He clenched his jaw. "Did he say that to you?"

She swallowed. It was painful admitting the truth. "He didn't have to, Tate. I could see it in his eyes. In the way he looked at me. All the life went out of them."

He made a clucking sound with his tongue. "Then he's not worth a single second more of your time."

She could see the raw emotion on her brother's face. It mirrored how she felt inside. Her throat clogged up. "That's not fair. I was the one who wasn't honest. No matter how I justified it at the time, it was wrong of me."

Tate rocked back on his heels, his silver-tipped cowboy boots glinting in the sun. He jammed his fists into his front pockets.

"Any man would be blessed to have you." He gazed off into the distance, his expression steely. "I worry about you, little sis. And it has nothing to do with you being in a wheelchair. You've worn your emotions on your sleeve ever since you were a kid. It kills me to think of someone hurting you."

"It's part of being alive. It happens when you live

life." She shrugged. "Let's face it. It comes with the territory. Even tough lawmen like you aren't immune to it."

Tate swung his gaze back in her direction. His eyes were moist. "You've always been a wise soul, do you know that? Even when we were kids and I was trying to protect you from the world, you always had a strong head on your shoulders. You never really needed me to fight your battles, did you?"

Holly chuckled as memories of her overprotective brother ran through her mind. "Nope, I didn't. But I always loved the fact that you cared enough to be my protector. It made me feel special."

"I'll never give up that role, you know," Tate said with a smirk. "It's a lifelong assignment."

Holly playfully rolled her eyes. "I can't wait till you and Cassidy get married and have a house full of kids. You'll be so busy chasing after them you won't have time to watch over me."

The thought of it made her a little wistful. Would she ever have a husband and a house full of kids? Or would she be relegated to the role of spinster auntie? Even before the accident, she'd always dreamed of rocking a baby to sleep in her arms. Now that might never happen. Was it realistic to dream of things that might not come to pass?

"It's hard to believe we're finally getting married." His larger-than-life grin was threatening to take over his entire face. It was nice to see Tate so overjoyed and on the verge of having all his dreams come to fruition. For a few minutes the two of them simply savored the moment, basking in the promise of tomorrow. Each and every day, Holly found great inspiration in Tate and Cassidy's love story. It kept her hoping and dreaming and praying. Perhaps she, too, would find her happily ever after.

"By the way, Dylan's not running." She tried to keep her tone conversational, despite the rapid quickening of her pulse. "For the next few months, anyway, he's sticking around in West Falls."

Her brother raised an eyebrow. "So what does that mean for the two of you?"

"We're just friends," she said. "I even told him to apply for a job here at the ranch. He's plenty qualified."

Tate furrowed his brow. "You're okay with him working here?"

She nodded her head vigorously. "I think it would be great. Hopefully I'll get the chance to win back his trust, if he'll allow me to."

Even though her statement was technically true about being in the friend zone with Dylan, she couldn't deny the rush of adrenaline she felt at the mere thought of him. Dylan Hart, her gorgeous, green-eyed pen pal. Her brave soldier. The man who'd traveled all the way from Oklahoma to see her, based on the connection they'd established.

For a woman who'd fought tooth and nail to rebuild her life after losing the ability to walk, it didn't feel good to feel so conflicted. She wished she could turn back time and rewrite all the letters she'd sent to Dylan. This time around she wouldn't hesitate to tell him the truth. Pressing her eyes closed, she prayed that she might have the opportunity to show Dylan she was the kind of woman he'd believed her to be before he'd arrived in West Falls.

Chapter Four

Dylan revved the engine of his truck, hoping the loud noise would rid his mind of all the chaotic thoughts swirling around him. The urge to leave Horseshoe Bend Ranch felt overwhelming. He slammed his hand against the steering wheel, letting out a low groan as he did so. Frustration speared him. Why would God allow a young girl to lose the use of her legs? Why did things like this happen?

The feelings of helplessness roared through him like thunder. It was the same question he'd pondered when Benji and Simon Akol had been killed in such a senseless, violent way. Where was He that day? In the days following Benji's and Simon's deaths, he'd been flat on his back, recovering from a broken neck, a hairline skull fracture and facial lacerations. For endless hours he'd replayed the explosion in his mind—the wreckage, the blood, the cries of pain, which still rang out in his ears. All the while he'd had no clue that two members of his squad had been killed, wiped out in a single deadly blast. His focus had been on staying alive.

Dark memories swept over him, threatening to take him to a place he didn't want to revisit. He'd tried so hard to forget the feelings of despair that had consumed him in the days and weeks after the bomb blast. And the fear of the unknown. He didn't want to lash out at God, not when he'd come so far on his spiritual journey. Although he still had a ways to go, he knew he'd turned a corner two and a half years ago. There was no way he was going back to that place in time when he'd been a nonbeliever.

Pressing his eyes closed, he tried to stop the flood of images from rushing through his mind. He didn't like to go back to those moments when dread had been ever present. It made him feel vulnerable and weak and not in control of his own destiny.

Son, you may never walk again. The military chaplain had clasped his hand and broken the news to him in the most compassionate way possible. He'd completely broken down, unable to comprehend a life without the use of his legs. During the bleakest days of his life, his mother had been at his side. They'd prayed together, asking God to grant him mercy and healing. In the end, once all the swelling subsided, he'd experienced sensation in his toes. From there he'd endured months of physical therapy, resulting in his regaining 100 percent function.

As the beautiful West Falls landscape passed by his window, a feeling of uncertainty grabbed hold of him. *What am I doing here? I thought by coming to West Falls I was following a path that would lead me toward the next chapter of my life.* Had this entire journey been nothing more than a pipe dream? A rash, foolish mistake?

The downtown area of West Falls was a vibrant section filled with quaint businesses. It looked like something one might see on a festive postcard. Colorful awnings, old-fashioned lampposts, kids skipping along the sidewalk. The Bowlarama caught his eye. Bowling had been one of his favorite pastimes as a kid growing up in Madden. For some reason Holly's image flashed before his eyes, and he wondered if she bowled. Was it even possible?

The cream-and-purple sign advertising the Falls Diner beckoned him like a beacon. West Falls was a far cry from the town he'd grown up in. Everyone greeted him with a warm hello or a smile in his direction. Many eyed him with curiosity. It didn't offend him one bit since the townsfolk seemed hospitable, not standoffish. No one made him feel like an outsider, something he'd been feeling for most of his life. It was a unique experience to have the welcome mat rolled out for him.

For Dylan, walking through the doors of the diner felt like stepping into another world. Delightful aromas wafted in the air as a pink-haired waitress poured coffee into nice-size mugs and chatted amiably with customers. Salmon-colored seats and aqua menus jumped out at him. The rhythmic beat of a blues band emanated from the jukebox. He looked down at a black-and-white parquet floor so clean he could almost see his reflection.

"Couldn't resist the smell, could you?" The gravelly voice drew his attention toward the counter area where Doc Sampson stood watching him. He wore a snowy apron with the word *Doc* emblazoned in red across the front. With a head full of white hair, warm brown eyes and a kindly expression, he was the quintessential small-town proprietor.

"I have to admit, you had me as soon as I spotted your sign." He patted his stomach. "I'm starving. What do you recommend?"

"Take a seat, son," Doc said as he gestured toward the counter. "How about the blue plate special with all the trimmings? It's the best buffalo chicken and sweet-potato fries you'll ever eat."

He slid onto the stool, feeling like a little kid again as he eyed one of the waitresses making a milk shake in the blender. "Sure. Sounds great, Mr. Sampson." In fact, it sounded so amazing his stomach began to grumble noisily. He hadn't eaten a bite since this morning. His eagerness to meet Holly had trumped his legendary appetite.

"What's with the Mr. Sampson business? Everyone around these parts calls me Doc."

He nodded his head in agreement. "Doc it is, then. And the blue plate special will do just fine."

"Coming right up, son." He studied Dylan for a moment, his silver brows furrowed. "I don't mean to pry, but I heard you were out at Horseshoe Bend Ranch. Were you looking for a job? I know they're looking for a few ranch hands. I'd be happy to put in a good word for you with the foreman, Malachi Finley."

Dylan tried to stuff down a feeling of discomfort. Doc Sampson seemed like a great guy, but after living in a gossipy town like Madden, he wasn't interested in revisiting the experience. It was only his first day in town, yet rumors about his comings and goings were already swirling around like dust on a windy day.

"No, I wasn't looking for a job, although I do need one," he acknowledged in a tone much lighter than his current mood. Doc was his landlord after all, and he needed to keep things cordial between them. "I went out there to meet my friend, Holly. She corresponded with me while I was in Afghanistan. It's because of her that I'm here in West Falls."

Doc's face lit up, and he let out a loud whoop of excitement. "Holly Lynch! She's one of my favorite people." He grinned at Dylan. "I imagine it was nice to finally meet her."

He hesitated, not sure how to answer the question. It hadn't been a good feeling to be played for a fool by Holly and Cassidy. On the other hand, he couldn't ignore all she'd meant to him over the past year. He couldn't forget what it felt like to hold one of her letters in his hand and to know someone cared, other than his mom, whether he lived or died. Warm sentiments didn't just evaporate in an instant, especially not the type of tight bond he and Holly had forged.

"I didn't know she was in a wheelchair." The words tumbled out of his lips before he could rein them back in. He was still grappling with Holly's lie, still unsure what to make of it all.

Doc's shoulders sagged, and he let out a deep sigh. "The poor thing lost the use of her legs before she even got a chance to spread her wings and fly." He shook his head as if trying to rid himself of the memories. "After the accident it felt like an earthquake hit this town. It was hard on the roses—that's what everyone calls her and her three friends—but Holly had it the worst. She had to learn to live life in a totally different way. No riding horses, no driving, no independence." His slight frame was racked by a huge shudder. "She struggled at first, but with her family and an abundance of faith, she pulled herself up by her bootstraps. That young lady is an inspiration." Doc winked at him and headed through the swinging doors into the kitchen.

Doc's heartfelt words about Holly nudged themselves straight into the center of his heart. He'd always known she was special. In a million years he could never convey all she'd done to keep his mind focused on living and making it back home rather than on the death and devastation he'd encountered on his last tour of duty. Her lively, warm letters had served as a lifeline, reminding him of everything he'd be coming back to in the States. And now he was discovering she'd had to climb mountains in her own life in order to overcome tragedy.

If he was being honest with himself, the urge to stick around West Falls had everything to do with Holly and the bond they'd forged. The idea of Holly bravely rebuilding her life in the aftermath of the accident made him want to get to know her in a way he hadn't been able to through their letters. Suddenly, staying in town had nothing to with practicality. He wanted to discover firsthand everything he possibly could about Holly Lynch.

The early-morning sun cast its stunning rays over the pastoral landscape. A calm feeling settled over him as he drove down the country lane. All he could see on the horizon was a cloudless sky the color of a robin's egg.

It was shaping up to being a beautiful October day in West Falls. If he lived to be a hundred, he would never tire of this perfect, sacred land. Thankfully, he was miles and miles away from IEDs, missiles and military strikes. For the first time in a long time he didn't have to think about whether or not this day would be his last. He wouldn't have to struggle to breathe the dank, fetid air. Ever since he'd left Afghanistan, his prayers had been full of mercy and protection for the soldiers he'd left behind. Husbands, mothers, brothers, friends— each and every one of them yearning to make it home to their loved ones.

Without warning, Horseshoe Bend Ranch came into spectacular view. Once again he allowed himself to take it all in. The raw beauty of the land rendered him speechless. It went on for acres and acres, as far as the eye could see. Green, verdant, unspoiled land. Even though Oklahoma had some breathtaking vistas, he'd never laid eyes on anything so pristine and majestic. He couldn't help but think that the Lord had left his finger-prints all over this spread. His chest swelled at the idea of one day owning his own cattle ranch, a dream he'd nurtured since he was a small boy. What would it feel like, he wondered, to experience the sense of pride as-sociated with building up the land into a thing of raw beauty and distinction?

After talking to Doc yesterday, he'd decided to speak to the foreman about being hired on as a ranch hand. It was hard to ignore that he was sorely in need of a job. And Horseshoe Bend Ranch was hiring.

The Lord will provide. His mother's velvety voice rang in his ears, instantly bringing him back to his upbringing in Oklahoma. If he had a dollar for every time Mama had uttered that sentiment, he'd be a millionaire. More times than not, money and food had been scarce, and they'd lived on the edge of poverty. Finally, in an act of humility, his mother had reached out to his father for financial help, which he'd immediately given. Although things had quickly improved after that, Dylan was left with a bitter taste in his mouth about accepting money from the father who didn't acknowledge him. It amounted to little more than charity. For so long he'd struggled with the notion of not being good enough. He'd been fighting to prove otherwise ever since.

After entering the gates, he traveled down a gravel-filled road. When he reached the fork in the road, he turned to the left as Doc had instructed. He glanced over to his right, catching sight of the sprawling main house. Had it just been yesterday he'd been sipping sweet tea inside those walls? He wondered where Holly was at the moment and what she was doing. Even though Holly had given him the go-ahead to seek employment on her family's ranch, he wondered if she might change her mind. Perhaps it would be awkward under the circumstances. Suddenly, he felt himself second-guessing his decision. Should he just turn the truck around and head back to town?

"Too late to turn back now." He glanced down at his bearded dragon, who was sitting in his carrier looking happy to be along for the ride. Leo enjoyed hanging out with him and he didn't mind the swaying movement. Dylan could always tell when he was happy, as well as the times when he wasn't. Being alone for long periods didn't seem to suit him. Rather than leave Leo

by himself, he'd decided to bring him on his trip out
to the ranch. Lizards thrived in hot desertlike weather,
so being stuck in a carrier on a warm October morning wasn't a problem. He looked down at the piece of
paper in his hand. Doc had scribbled down the name
for him. Malachi Finley.

According to Doc, he was the one who did all the hiring at the ranch. He pulled up to the stables and parked
his truck alongside a few cars. Knowing he'd come too
far to turn back, he unfolded his long legs and exited.
The stable door was wide-open, giving him a clear view
of two ranch hands who were trying to rein in a buck-
ing miniature horse.

"Are either of you Malachi Finley?"

Neither man bothered to look up. One of them gestured outside. "Nope. He's out in the corral."

"Thanks," Dylan said as he turned on his heel and
made his way back outside. If he wasn't here on such
pressing business, he might have been tempted to stay
in the stables and watch the struggle between the miniature horse and the ranchers. Something told him that
the spirited animal might win the battle. As he stepped
out into the sunlight, he had to raise his arm across his
face to protect himself from the glare. Because of the
rays shining directly in his face, he could make out
only two indistinct figures—one astride a horse, the
other standing close by. The first thing he noticed was
the glint of blond hair shimmering in the sun. Goose
bumps broke out on his arms as the realization hit him
hard. It was Holly.

She was seated on an alabaster, medium-size horse.
A Native American man, who he assumed to be Mala-

chi, stood by her side, holding the lead rope and directing the horse. Holly's focus was 100 percent on the task at hand. Her hands were clutching the bridle. She was so focused that she didn't seem to notice he was thirty feet away, observing her.

Only a moment ago, he'd deliberated as to whether he should even be at Horseshoe Bend Ranch. But now he was transfixed by the sight of Holly on her horse. She looked scared. Even from where he was standing, way across the yard, he could see the signs of it. Her blue eyes were open wide, and she was blinking, giving her the look of a frightened owl. Seeing her discomfort made him want to do something—anything—to help her. It made him want to jump the fence and ride to her rescue. Malachi was being gentle with her. Maybe he was going too easy on her, he realized. No doubt he was well-meaning, but Holly wasn't making any progress. She resembled a statue perched on a horse. Her head was moving back and forth, as if she was arguing with Malachi. Not a single thing about her indicated she was happy or feeling joyful. Hadn't Holly written to him about her love of horses? Shouldn't she at least be smiling?

"Holly, you can't show him you're scared. If he senses it, it'll spook him," he called out. None of this was his business, but he couldn't just sit back and watch her fall apart.

She glanced in his direction, her eyes opening even wider as soon as she spotted him. Wobbling a little in her seat, she let out cry of alarm. Malachi steadied her, and for the first time, he could see the special saddle she was using. There was a belt attached to the saddle that was looped around her waist, as well as a padded back to the saddle. Between Malachi and the saddle, there really hadn't been any real danger of her falling. But, as he well knew, fear lived in one's mind.

"Spook him? I'm the one whose hands are trembling. He's got the easy part," she yelled back.

"Malachi, do you mind if I come inside?" he called out. He didn't want to step on his toes, but helping Holly feel at ease was his primary concern. He watched as Malachi looked up at Holly, his dark eyes questioning her. Holly gave him a quick nod. Malachi gestured him in.

Dylan entered the arena, his movements calm and easy. The last thing he wanted to do was startle Holly's horse. At the moment, both rider and horse seemed unsettled. When he edged closer, he was able to see the elastic bands attached to the stirrup. He imagined they were being used to stabilize her feet. As soon as he reached her side, he was able to read the saying on her shirt—I'm Paralyzed. There's Nothing Wrong With My Hearing. The corners of his mouth twitched, but he didn't want Holly to see his amusement. She needed to dig down deep and take control of the situation. There was no time for distractions.

Without saying a word, Malachi moved a few steps away and folded his arms across his chest. It was clear to Dylan that he wanted to be close enough where he could still keep an eye on the situation. He didn't blame him. As far as Malachi was concerned, he was a stranger. There hadn't even been time to introduce himself. What would he have said anyway? "Hi, I'm

Dylan, Holly's pen pal from Afghanistan"? Something told him Malachi wasn't big on chitchat.

Dylan looked up at Holly, immediately noticing the tension lines creasing her pretty features. Resisting the impulse to smooth away those crinkles, he tried to assess the situation. He didn't know whether this was her fourth time back in the saddle or her fortieth. At the Bar M, he'd worked with plenty of disabled riders, most of whom were missing limbs or suffering from war injuries. They called it therapeutic riding.

Because of his experience in Afghanistan, he knew what fear looked like, up close and personal. At the moment, anxiety held Holly firmly in its grip.

"Sometimes life's not easy." He threw the words out like a challenge, wanting to remind Holly of everything she was too scared to see right now. She'd written those words to him when he'd been full of despair and dejected, having been inundated with bad news about failed missions, roadside bombs and fallen soldiers. Holly and her sweet, spirited letters always served as a shining beacon of hope in the darkness. Now, in some small way, he wanted to give back to her a little bit of inspiration.

"Hey, it's not fair to use my own words against me!" she protested. The beginnings of a small smile hovered on her lips.

Pleasure filled him at the sight of it. She was starting to relax. Her posture didn't look so rigid anymore, and her features weren't so strained.

"What's your horse's name? He's a beauty, that's for sure." He reached out and stroked the stallion's glorious mane. He'd missed being on a ranch—all the sights, smells, sounds and the glorious animals. Being with horses filled a piece of his soul as nothing else could.

"His name is Sundance. He's a Camarillo."

He let out a low whistle. Camarillo horses, categorized by their pure-white appearance, were a rare breed of horse. Although he knew of their existence, he'd never seen one until now. It shouldn't surprise him since, according to Doc, Horseshoe Bend Ranch was among the most successful horse-breeding operations in the country. No doubt the Lynches could afford the best horses money could buy.

She thoughtfully studied him. "What brought you out here today?"

Dylan met her gaze, startled by the jolt he felt as he looked into her eyes. "Doc convinced me to swing by and see Malachi about a job, since I'm sticking around for a while." He shrugged, feeling a bit sheepish.

"Why'd you decide to ride today?" he asked, quickly veering off the topic.

She shot him a look of frustration. "It's one of my goals. I've been trying to get back into riding for years. Before the accident I rode all the time. Every time I get up here for my lesson, I freeze up." She pointed her chin in Malachi's direction. "Every single time. Just ask Malachi."

"You're afraid." His words were simple and to the point. Even a blind man could sense her fear. It was palpable.

She vehemently shook her head, blond hair tumbling over her eyes. "I love horses, Dylan. I'm not afraid. I just—"

Their gazes locked, and he could see stark terror

looking back at him. He didn't want to push her too hard, since she already seemed to be on edge. She looked as if all the steam had left her. He deliberately softened his voice.

"It's understandable, you know. You don't need to feel ashamed about it. Being involved in the accident, not riding for so long… It's bound to mess with your confidence." Compassion flared within him. "I know what it feels like. When I became injured, I was laid up in a military hospital for months. By the time they discharged me and I'd redeployed, I was a mess. Physically, I healed." He tapped two fingers against his temple. "But mentally, I was scared to death of every loud noise and shadow."

Holly bit her lip and looked away. "I guess I am a little scared. Not of the horses," she quickly added. "It's been such a long time since I've done this. Almost a lifetime ago. I just don't want to fail at it again."

"You can do this, Holly," he said in a firm voice. "I know you can."

She studied him for a moment, her eyes roaming over his face. He watched her take a deep breath, then sit up straight in her saddle, shoulders back, her mouth pressed in a thin line. With a simple nod of her head, she let Malachi know she was ready to try again. Soundlessly, Malachi appeared at Sundance's side, his eyes carefully trained on Holly. Sensing Malachi possessed some special training he didn't have, Dylan retreated a few steps but still kept his gaze trained on horse and rider.

In a soothing voice, Holly began talking to Sundance, uttering words he couldn't hear. She gently grazed her knuckles against his temple. The stallion nickered softly in response. Holly picked up the reins and instructed Sundance to move. The horse obeyed, gracefully moving into a simple trot. Holly patted his side forcefully, urging him to trot a little faster. Dylan held his breath as she cantered around the corral. Although her pace wasn't fast by any means, it was a clear victory for Holly as she settled into the natural rhythms of riding. Malachi hovered nearby, his eyes trained on both horse and rider, ready to jump in at any moment.

After twenty minutes or so, Holly began showing signs of fatigue. She slowed Sundance to a halt, then gestured to Malachi, who was at her side in seconds. He watched as they headed toward a ramp and a wheelchair, both set off to the side of the corral. Strangely, in the past half hour, he'd allowed himself to forget about Holly's disability. All he'd wanted to do was rush in and make things better. But now the reality of her situation hit him squarely in the stomach. Feelings of helplessness washed over him. Fear grabbed him by the throat. As Malachi helped Holly off Sundance, he squared his shoulders and turned away, swallowing hard as memories of his own stint in a wheelchair bombarded him. He fisted his palms, determined not to go into a dark place.

"Atta girl. I knew you'd get back in the saddle one of these days," a deep masculine voice rang out as long legs began walking toward them.

Dylan held his hand up to block out the glare from the sun, catching a glimpse of dark hair and a strong jaw. Holly lit up the moment the tall, broad-shouldered man came into view. He felt a twinge of discomfort, knowing there was someone who could make Holly shine like the sun.

The dark-haired man stopped midstride, giving him the once-over as he planted himself next to him. Holly adroitly wheeled over to them, making introductions as she reached their side.

"Tate, this is Dylan Hart. Dylan, this is my brother, Sheriff Tate Lynch."

Dylan stuck out his hand, and for a moment, the sheriff seemed to hesitate before putting his hand out and vigorously shaking it. His gold badge glinted in the sun, serving as a reminder that Tate Lynch ran things in West Falls.

"He's come to talk to Malachi about a job on the ranch." She looked toward Malachi, who'd just walked over and joined them. "Malachi, officially meet Dylan."

Malachi nodded his head almost imperceptibly in his direction.

Tate jutted his chin toward him. His blue eyes sized him up, not giving a thing away. "Holly mentioned you have some ranch experience."

"Yeah, I spent summers working as a ranch hand at the Bar M Ranch in Madden, Oklahoma. You name it, I did it. Breaking in horses. Wrangling. Roping. Doctoring livestock. Calving. Fence repair."

Tate nodded, his eyes alight with interest. "I've heard of the Bar M. Nice little operation. I remember meeting the owner a few years back at a cattle auction. McDermott, isn't it?"

Dylan tensed up the moment at the mention of his father's name. He allowed himself to relax. It wasn't as if anyone would ever guess the connection. "Yes, that's right. R. J. McDermott. I cut my teeth there and learned a lot."

"He's got a nice way with horses," Malachi added. "I'd say he knows his way around a ranch." Dylan blinked in surprise. Malachi hadn't said two words to him, yet he'd clearly been taking stock of him the whole time.

With a lot of eyebrow raising and head nods, Tate and Malachi seemed to be communicating to one another without uttering a single word.

Tate folded his arms across his chest. "We just had two of our ranch hands up and quit on us, so we need to bring someone on right away to fill the slack. Most folks say it's a nice place to work."

"I think Tate's offering you a job," Holly said in a dry tone. "If he ever gets around to it."

"Is that right?" Dylan asked, shooting a grin in Holly's direction. Joy swept through him at the prospect of being offered a job on his own merits. Other than his service in the military, the only employment he'd ever secured was at the Bar M, and that had been due to his father. In the end, that hadn't worked out too well.

Tate glanced over at Malachi, who nodded his head and added, "The job is yours if you want it."

Gratitude swelled inside him. Who wouldn't want to work at this magnificent ranch, this little slice of paradise? He reached out and shook Malachi's hand. "Thanks for the offer. I'd be happy to come on board."

He couldn't resist looking over at Holly. Her expression bore no hint of any discomfort. If she was surprised by the turn of events, she didn't show it. She looked serene, as if all was right in her world. It seemed that having successfully ridden Sundance had left Holly with a permanent glow on her face.

Thank You, Lord. Thanks for giving Holly back a small piece of something she lost. And for giving me this amazing opportunity at Horseshoe Bend Ranch. I still don't know why You called me to West Falls, but at the moment I'm feeling mighty grateful to be here.

Having Dylan show up unexpectedly at the ranch left Holly with mixed emotions. At first she'd been embarrassed by having him witness her pitiful attempts at riding Sundance. Her lack of finesse was painful, particularly since she'd once been a top-notch rider. Her childhood bedroom had been littered with blue ribbons and trophies. She'd loved galloping across her family's massive acreage with the wind flying through her hair. Sometimes she missed riding so much it caused a physical pain in her body. It was a relentless ache in her soul that wouldn't quit. At times she missed having the use of her legs so much she started to believe she felt normal sensation in her lower extremities.

When Dylan came striding into the corral looking every inch a cowboy on a mission, she'd been surprised and full of jitters. He'd quickly made her feel at ease, soothing not only her but the horse, as well. With his strong, gentle hands and soft voice, he'd made everything better. In his presence she'd felt safe. Not many people made her feel that way. His actions also showed her that he wasn't harboring any ill will toward her, even though he'd distanced himself once Malachi helped her dismount.

Tate's eyes were full of questions as his gaze shifted

between her and Dylan. Not that she didn't have her own. There were so many times over the past year she'd felt there might be something more than friendship brewing between them. And having Dylan show up in West Falls seemed to confirm he was leaning toward more than a platonic relationship. Until he'd discovered she was in a wheelchair. Until she'd pretended to be somebody she wasn't.

A little while ago Dylan had disappeared into the stables with Tate and Malachi, no doubt to talk shop and get the particulars about his new job. A part of her ached to tag along so she could show Dylan around the stables herself and introduce him to Fiddlesticks, Picasso and all the other horses. If her parents had been at the ranch, she would have introduced them to Dylan as well, but they were out of town at a horse auction and would be on the road indefinitely.

Wanting to give Dylan his space, she'd stayed outside to give Sundance some apple treats and water before grooming him. As she worked her way with a comb through Sundance's tail, she heaped praise on the magnificent stallion.

"Hey, I thought you might like to meet someone." When she looked up, Dylan was standing there holding a lizard in his arms. A dark cowboy hat was now perched on his head. The bearded dragon was a light green color with dark brown spots scattered across his back. He was beautiful.

"It's Leo! Oh, he's amazing," she gushed. She maneuvered herself away from where Sundance was tethered to his post, not wanting him to be frightened by the lizard. "And he's so much bigger than I imagined."

Dylan laughed. "Yeah, he is, isn't he? He's about a foot now and still growing. I have to make a stop at the market so I can stock up on the veggies and fruits he likes to eat, not to mention I have to find some silk-worms and grubs."

Hearing Dylan talk about Leo was like listening to a parent crow over a child. He was acting like a proud papa. And she didn't blame him one bit. Leo was fantastic. She leaned forward in her chair, anxious to get a better look at the lizard.

"Can I hold him? I promise I'll be careful."

His eyes widened at her request. A slow, wide smile began to break out on his face. "Sure thing. Just hold out both of your palms to support him."

She held out her hands and Dylan adroitly handed Leo over to her. The first thing she noticed was his solid weight. "Whoa. He's a big boy!"

"You got that right. Make sure you support his front arms with your fingers. You can put him in your lap if you want. Might make it easier."

Holly placed Leo in her lap and ran her finger down his back, surprised at the rough texture of his skin. Leo just sat there bobbing his head.

"Most people are a little nervous about holding Leo."

"Not me," she said with a grin. "He's adorable. And he's such a sweetheart to let a stranger hold him."

"Leo's an attention hound. The more he gets, the better he likes it." Dylan's face held a pleased expression. "Bearded dragons get a bad rap. They're actually very gentle creatures despite their name."

"Aw, you're just misunderstood, aren't you? Don't worry, Leo. I don't judge by appearances," she cooed.

Leo lay snuggled in her lap as if he planned to stay for a while. She wouldn't mind a bit if he did. "I think he likes me."

"Wouldn't surprise me a bit." Dylan crossed his arms across his chest and studied the two of them. The satisfied expression on his face only served to enhance his good looks. "Leo has good taste."

Dylan's compliment washed over her like a gentle breeze. The wind kicked up a bit, blowing her hair all around her face. As it was, it already had a habit of being on the unruly side. She didn't need the elements to make things worse. *Especially in front of Dylan,* a little voice whispered. Without warning, he reached out and brushed a few strands out of her eyes, his fingers gently grazing her cheek in the process. His touch was warm and tender, making her want to burrow her face against his palm. She looked up at him, and as their eyes met, she felt something electric hovering in the air. There was a slight tension that hadn't been there a moment ago. It crackled and buzzed around them.

Dylan took a step backward, his eyes flickering with an emotion she couldn't decipher. "I should really be getting back to town. I've barely gotten settled in, and I'm supposed to be reporting to work tomorrow."

"I'm thrilled you'll be working at Horseshoe Bend Ranch." She smiled up at him, hoping he felt as good about his decision as she did. "And in case I didn't make it clear yesterday, I'm happy you decided to stay in West Falls."

"Thanks for saying so, Holly. I'm glad to be here." Dylan nodded his head and sent her a lazy smile before tipping his cowboy hat in her direction and turning to leave.

As he walked away, she wavered between joy and discomfort. There was no denying she felt a tremendous pull in his direction. Her insides did flip-flops whenever he was nearby. She felt breathless around him, as if she'd ridden Sundance through the countryside for a whole hour without stopping. Just one glance from him caused her to feel slightly off-kilter. It had been years and years since she'd felt anything like it, and even then, it had been nothing more than a high school romance.

On the other hand, having him nearby didn't help get him out of her mind. And she knew the more she thought about him, the harder it would be for her when he left town. He'd made it pretty clear he wasn't sticking around past the duration of his lease with Doc.

Even though things were now way more complicated between them, he was still there, firmly rooted in her heart. Over the past year, she'd read and reread his letters, almost to the point of memorizing every word and detail. In her mind, there had been an unspoken closeness between them, one that hinted of a future together. Somehow, their physical separation had allowed her to forget the wide chasm between them and all the reasons why they were so very ill suited for one another.

Every time she glanced in his direction, it became even more crystal clear. Dylan was the embodiment of the perfect male specimen. Tall. Rugged. Muscular. The personification of health and good living. Although she'd gotten used to being different a long time ago, those differences were magnified when she was side by side with Dylan.

She couldn't remember ever feeling such an intense longing for someone, one that reached all the way down to her toes. It was an exhilarating, breathless feeling. And as much as it excited her, it also frightened her. She'd been without male companionship for so long that she'd convinced herself she was fine without love in her life. With his piercing green eyes and laid-back demeanor, Dylan was quickly showing her how wrong she'd been in her thinking. *Just fine* wasn't enough. She wanted more than that. Dylan's presence in West Falls was igniting a whole new world of possibilities. For the first time since she was a little girl, she was dreaming of happily ever afters.

And she had the feeling, if she wasn't really careful, that in a few months' time, Dylan was going to leave West Falls with her heart firmly nestled in the palm of his hand.

Chapter Five

Twenty-four hours had passed since her riding lesson, and Holly found herself gritting her teeth as she battled waves of pain. She maneuvered herself over the threshold of her house, then quickly wheeled herself down the ramp and made her way over to her van. She paused for a moment, gritting her teeth against the ripples of pain threatening to overwhelm her. The sensations pulsating through her body were agonizing. Her legs were tingling as if they were on fire. Her arms were burning. Sucking in a deep breath, she reminded herself to breathe.

She didn't have time for this, not when she was supposed to be at Main Street Church in fifteen minutes, speaking to the youth group about distracted driving. Her motivational-speaking gigs were very important to her. As well as providing her with independence and an income, it gave her an opportunity to give back to the community she loved so much. At the moment, the chances of her making it to the church on time were getting smaller by the second.

She inhaled, slowly breathing in through her nose. There were so many ups and downs with her pain levels. Yesterday she'd felt fine. She'd even made her way over to Cassidy's house to apologize for her careless words. Over chamomile tea and shortbread cookies they'd shed a few tears and hugged it out. Now, less than twenty-four hours later, her body was racked with pain.

"Hold it together. *This too shall pass,*" she whispered, willing the agony to disappear. As it was, she could hardly focus, and there was absolutely no way she could lift herself into the van. She just didn't have the strength to push past the pain. Tears pricked her eyes as she imagined having to call Pastor Blake and cancel her speaking engagement. She'd fought so hard to not be limited by her disability, and yet here she was, sidelined by it. She shared a very special relationship with Pastor Blake. Not only was he Cassidy's father but he was also the one who'd led her back to her faith after the accident. The thought of disappointing him left her feeling dispirited.

"'Fear not, for I am with you.'" She repeated the words over and over again, firmly shutting her eyes to try to assuage the pain.

"Is everything okay over here?" Dylan's voice washed over her, making her forget for a moment about the agony coursing through her body. She heard the crunch of his cowboy boots on the pebbled driveway right before he popped into view. Dressed in a pair of dark jeans and an olive-colored T-shirt, he was a welcome sight.

Holly grimaced as waves of pain enveloped her. As

much as she didn't want Dylan to pity her, she couldn't hide that she was hurting.

"Yep, everything's fine." Somehow she managed to choke the words out.

Green eyes skimmed over her like lasers. "No, it's not. Something's wrong. You're all tensed up. You're suffering, aren't you, Holly?"

Dylan was frowning at her as if he knew she was trying to pull the wool over his eyes. Despite everything, he still connected with her so well. He was so in tune with her that he sensed something was amiss. Although it felt good to see that their connection hadn't been severed, it was a little unnerving at the moment to meet his probing gaze head-on. His eyes emitted such intensity. It felt as if he could see much more than she wanted to reveal. She broke eye contact, not wanting him to see the distress radiating from her eyes. If she could just have a moment to herself, she could dig in her purse for her medication, then call Pastor Blake and cancel her speaking engagement. The last thing she wanted was for Dylan to see her as a helpless invalid.

"Just having some nerve pain. I'll be all right."

The only thing she could do at the moment to alleviate the pain was to massage her legs and take another pill. Despite her inability to walk, she still had sensation and partial movement in her legs. Earlier this morning she'd taken her medication, but it seemed to be having no effect on her symptoms. She began kneading her legs with her fingers, willing the pain to go away. This harrowing side effect of the accident was unpredictable and jarring.

Dylan frowned. "It looks pretty bad. I can tell by the way you're clenching your teeth."

He got low to the ground so he was sitting on his haunches. Dylan reached for her hand, clasping it firmly in his. His touch felt comforting, like an infusion of warmth invading her body.

"Tell me what I can do. There must be something, Holly. Anything," he said, his tone urgent.

She blinked away tears of frustration. Time was slipping through her fingers, and she was still no closer to being able to get in the van. And even if she did somehow manage to get in the driver's seat, she wasn't confident she'd be able to block out the pain so she could safely drive into town. Her options were rapidly evaporating.

"I'm supposed to be at Main Street Church in ten minutes for a speaking engagement, but I don't think I can drive. I need to call Pastor Blake and cancel. He's been so wonderful about finding me outlets as a motivational speaker."

"There's no need to cancel, Holly, unless you're feeling too poorly to go. I can drive you over there. It'll take about fifteen minutes, but I'll get you there."

"Can you?" she asked, relief flooding through her at the offer. With her parents in Kentucky looking at horses and Tate on the clock at the sheriff's office, she didn't have many options. Malachi was notorious for not owning a cell phone, so even though he was just down the road at the stables, reaching him was impossible.

"I don't want to put you out." If Dylan was heading into work, she didn't want to take up his time. Under the circumstances, Malachi would be understanding, but she didn't want to make it appear as if Dylan were shirking his duties, especially as a new hire.

Dylan's brow furrowed. "Don't worry. It's fine. I was just heading back into town after working a shift when I spotted you over here. Don't ask me how I knew, but something didn't seem right. You were sitting there for quite a spell without getting into your van, and you were a little hunched over." He looked down at his dirt-stained shirt and chuckled. "I'm in need of a hot shower, so bear with me."

From where she was sitting, he looked pretty easy on the eyes, if a little rough around the edges. Having grown up on a ranch, she was used to cowboys in all their rugged glory. It would take a whole lot more than a grimy shirt and some smudges on his face to make Dylan look unappealing.

Realizing she was staring, she felt her cheeks redden. "You're going to have to lift me into the passenger seat, then put my chair in the back."

With a curt nod, Dylan said, "Let's do this." He stood up and brushed some dirt off his jeans. He went behind her chair and began pushing her toward his truck.

After pulling the door open on the passenger side, he turned back toward Holly. He reached down and placed his hands under one of her legs, then slid them underneath the other so he could scoop her up. Ever so gently, he raised her out of the wheelchair, pressing her firmly against his rock-solid chest. Slight fear kicked in. Although she trusted Dylan, being held in someone's arms was an extremely vulnerable position to be in. There were so few people in her life whom she trusted to carry her.

"Just don't drop me," she blurted, giving voice to her fears.

He drew her in closer. His grip tightened. The scent of hay and sandalwood rose to her nostrils.

"Everything's okay," he answered, his voice soft and soothing. "I'm not going to let anything happen to you. Wrap your arms around my neck."

With wide eyes Holly obeyed, her tight grip betraying her nervousness. "I've got you," he whispered in her ear, his lips grazing against her skin. "And there's no way I'm letting go."

As Dylan walked toward his truck, his mind was racing a few paces ahead of his footsteps. He wanted to be as gentle as possible when he placed her in the passenger seat of the car. A few seconds ago she'd seemed anxious, and he wanted her to feel at ease with him. He wanted to show her that her faith in him wasn't misguided. Even though his nerves were rattled by this huge responsibility and his breathing was a bit ragged, he wasn't going to let Holly down. After all, trust was a precious gift.

When he lowered her onto the seat, strands of golden hair brushed against his cheek. Her scent hovered in the air—a sweet perfumed smell reminiscent of sunshine and roses. She was shivering, no doubt in response to the pain, which sent his protective instincts into high gear. Unlike the other times he'd seen Holly, she looked more professional today. She'd ditched her humorously worded T-shirts for a bright blue button-down top and a dark pair of trousers. Silver-tipped cowboy boots peeked out from under the hem of her pants. She looked beautiful.

He made sure she was safely buckled in before he put her chair in the back, moved around to the driver's side and settled himself in. As they exited the gates of Horseshoe Bend Ranch, he shot a quick glance in her direction. "You look really nice today," he said, trying to make his voice sound casual.

She turned toward him, her cornflower-blue eyes widening at the compliment. It made him wonder if she wasn't used to receiving them or if she was just surprised he'd commented on her appearance. The corners of her perfectly shaped mouth turned up, instantly transforming into a glorious smile. Since he was so close to her, he got a good look at the light freckles scattered across her nose and cheeks. "Thanks," she said, smoothing down the front of her shirt. "Most of the kids come to this program after school, so I try to make an effort, even though I'm more comfortable in a T-shirt and jeans."

"Nothing wrong with that. It's my unofficial uniform," he said with a chuckle. "So how did you get started as a motivational speaker?"

"Well, I've kind of grown in to it. Right after the accident, I was pretty messed up." She darted a quick glance in his direction. "Emotionally, I mean, not just physically. I was angry at God for not sparing me the loss of my legs, so I floundered for a while, both spiritually and socially. Cassidy had been my best friend for most of my life, so when she left town without warning after the accident, I didn't have anyone to lean on.

My family was wonderful, but sometimes you just need your girlfriends."

The roses. The tight circle Doc had mentioned the other day at the diner.

Holly continued, "Jenna and Regina are two of my friends who were in the car wreck that night. Afterward they both retreated into their own shells, no doubt because of the circumstances of the accident. It was traumatic for all of us. There was so much fear and secrecy. It was the end of our innocence." She let out a deep sigh. "Our immaturity cost us all so much."

"You most of all." There was no question in his mind that Holly had paid the highest price of anyone. Everyone else had been able to carry on with their lives without permanent scars. Except Holly. Her injuries would last a lifetime.

"Most would say that, but I wasn't wearing a seat belt the night of the accident, Dylan. I'm embarrassed to admit that I was hanging out the window at the time of the crash."

Dylan tried to shutter his expression so Holly wouldn't see the shock roaring through him. *Hanging out the window of a moving vehicle?* He cleared his throat. "That doesn't sound like you, Holly. If you don't mind me asking, what made you do such a thing?"

She bowed her head. "No, I don't mind you asking. And you're right. It's not something I would do at this point in my life, but at eighteen years old, I was a bit of a risk taker, a free spirit of sorts. I was the one in the group who was always pushing the envelope." She shrugged. "You never think anything bad can happen to you when you're that age. You think you're invincible."

"You're right," he agreed, as images of his own youthful foolishness raced through his mind. "Been there, done that."

She let out a deep sigh. "My girlfriends and I were enjoying a fun night out on the town when we ran out of things to do. I guess we were bored. We'd played this game before called chicken, where whoever was driving would mess around with the car and veer into the other lane. I'm ashamed to say we thought it was entertaining. Cassidy was driving, and I was in the front passenger seat. I remember taking my seat belt off so I could hang out the window and feel the rain pour down on my face as I let out a few screams of frustration." He darted a glance at her, aching a little as he saw the bleak expression on her face. "My parents were really strict about my curfew, so I was chafing against their house rules. I thought they were treating me like a child. The car hit a slick patch in the rain and we crashed. Since Cassidy was driving, she bore the brunt of the blame and responsibility. We vowed among the four of us we'd never tell about our reckless behavior. It's only recently that we began telling the truth about that night."

Although Holly's tone was matter-of-fact, the actual details of the accident and its chilling aftermath were anything but routine. He couldn't seem to wrap his head around how quickly things had changed for Holly, how irrevocably her life had been transformed in a matter of minutes.

"And as a result, life as you'd known it ceased to exist," he said as a gnawing sensation tugged at his stomach. "You were forever changed."

Holly turned toward him, the corners of her mouth

hinting at the beginnings of a smile. "That's true. Nothing has been the same since that night. But believe it or not, I'm one of the fortunate ones. I could so easily have lost my life when I was ejected from the car. God was watching out for me even though I failed to watch out for myself."

"Wow. It's amazing you can be so…so at peace with it."

"Well, it didn't happen overnight. It took me a long time to come to that realization."

Chills raced along his spine at the thought of a battered and broken Holly, after being thrown from the car, lying on the road hovering between life and death. Hearing Holly's story was shocking and moving at the same time. One moment she'd been a typical teenager having a girls' night out. The next thing she knew she'd woken up in the hospital with catastrophic injuries. It was mind-blowing just thinking about all she'd endured. And everything she had to live with on a daily basis. His own experience with being paralyzed had been of such short duration that he couldn't compare his situation to Holly's. There were so many things that able-bodied people like himself were clueless about. He knew he wouldn't have handled things quite so well if the injuries he'd sustained in the bomb blast had been permanent. As it was, he'd been severely depressed and filled with uncertainty about his future. He'd lived in fear for months. Holly seemed to have navigated her way through her own terrible storm with grace and courage.

"Don't get me wrong. In the beginning I was bitter and apathetic. I kept asking myself why God had chosen me to be so horribly affected by the accident. I'm ashamed to admit it, but I kept wondering why the other girls had remained unscathed. That type of thinking did nothing to move me forward. One day I attended services at Main Street Church, and it was as if a light-bulb went off in my head when I heard Pastor Blake's sermon. I realized it was time to stop feeling sorry for myself and blaming God for my troubles. It was time to start living. After that, I committed myself not only to leading a more faith-driven life but to giving back to my community. This town has stood behind me every step of my journey, so it's only fitting that I talk to the teens about my own experience with reckless driving."

He nodded. "There's certainly a need for it. You hear about teen-driving fatalities all the time."

"Teenagers don't have fully formed brains, so decisions made on the spur of the moment can be life altering. I don't want to lecture them. I just want them to see with their own eyes what can happen when poor decision-making spirals out of control."

Holly was spot-on. Teens didn't want some know-it-all telling them the dos and don'ts of adolescence. That was a surefire way of losing an audience and having them block out anything anyone tried to tell them. He knew this all too well from his own experiences with eighteen-year-old recruits, who chafed at being told what to do. Over time they'd learned the value of listening to more experienced soldiers. Sometimes their very lives depended on it.

Something told him Holly made a powerful impression all on her own.

Fifteen minutes later, they arrived at Main Street Church. After Dylan parked the truck, he retrieved the wheelchair from the back, then scooped Holly up and settled her back in the chair. Having done it once before gave him the confidence to know he could handle it without complications. Once he was finished, Dylan stood on the curb, craning his neck up toward the towering structure. He remembered Holly writing him about the storm that had damaged the church's roof and toppled its historic steeple. Although the roof had been fully restored, the church was still missing its crowning glory. According to Holly, the church was having ongoing fund-raising events to pay for the costly repair. Little by little, she said, they were moving toward their goal. Even without the steeple, the house of worship was still magnificent.

A good-looking man with salt-and-pepper hair and a kind expression stood at the top of the stairs by the entrance. His slate-gray eyes were welcoming. A smile lit up his face. Dylan had a good hunch this was Pastor Blake, the inspiring man he'd heard so much about over the past year.

"Holly! So glad you could make it after all," he called out as Holly wheeled herself up the ramp and toward the entrance. "I was getting a little worried. You're usually the first one to arrive."

"Sorry, Pastor Blake. I'm running a few minutes late. I needed some help getting here today." She cast a glance in Dylan's direction, her eyes filled with gratitude. "Thankfully, my friend Dylan was able to help me out."

Pastor Blake heartily clapped him on the back. "We're mighty grateful to you, son. She's a bright ray of sunshine around here. The teens are already in the rec room waiting for her arrival."

"Let's get to it, then," Holly said with a grin as she sailed through the open door.

Pastor Blake chuckled and shook his head, then ushered Dylan inside the church. The interior was cool and dimly lit. After following Holly down the aisle, he stopped in his tracks, awed by the way the sunlight streamed like gold ribbons through the stained-glass windows, bathing the altar in natural light.

Pastor Blake paused beside him. "Beautiful, isn't it? Sometimes in the middle of the day I just sit down in one of the pews and enjoy a moment of reflection."

Dylan nodded. He didn't know what to say, even though the idea of enjoying a peaceful moment here appealed to him. It had been a long time since he'd been in God's house. He'd spent some time in the chapel at the hospital while he was recuperating from his injuries, but that had been the extent of it. It shamed him to acknowledge he hadn't lived up to his vow. At the time, he'd made a lot of promises about living a more spiritual life. He'd been so grateful to God for giving him back the use of his legs, so relieved that he didn't have to spend the rest of his life in a wheelchair, promises had flowed out of his mouth like quicksilver. As he walked behind Holly's wheelchair as she led the way to the recreation room, the irony struck him square in the chest. He'd been spared while Holly had been dealt a crushing blow.

Once they reached the hallway, the sounds of animated voices drifted toward them. The recreation room was a large-size area with a brightly colored mural on the wall. There were about twenty teenagers seated around the room. As soon as they spotted Holly, a roar went up in the place. Looking pleased with the warm reception, Holly introduced him to the group. Some of the girls sent him flirty looks and smiles so sweet they almost gave him a toothache. The boys seemed to be sizing him up, staring at him with curious gazes. He held up his hand in greeting before stepping aside and settling into a seat at the back of the room, right before Holly began speaking.

"Hi guys. It's nice to see so many people could make it. I know we've talked a lot about reckless driving, but today I want to talk about personal responsibility." She positioned herself right in the center of the room, where everyone had a good view of her sitting in her wheel-chair. "The way I see it, if you're a passenger in a car, you also have an obligation to make sure the driver is being safe. No texting. No drinking. No game playing. Bottom line…if the driver isn't being responsible, you're putting your own life in danger. Take it from me. It isn't worth it."

For the next half hour Holly went over different scenarios and had the teens role-play. Although a few of the teens were making jokes and goofing around, most of them were taking their assignments very seriously. Throughout, Holly handled herself in a professional manner, gently reining in the kids when they veered off track. She never sounded preachy or holier-than-thou. Authenticity rang out in every syllable. She'd clearly walked the walk, and the kids all knew it. The teens peppered her with questions about her own accident, and she painstakingly answered every one of them, even the ones that made his jaw drop. Her bravery and transparency were awe inspiring.

At the end of the session, a pretty dark-skinned girl raised her hand. "Sarah, do you have a question?" Holly asked, her attention focused solely on her.

"Miss Holly, we were talking before you got here about how we can give back to the community. So we—"

A tall boy with ginger hair and freckles chimed in. "We want to have a bake sale at school to help with the steeple fund."

"We know it probably won't make a dent in the overall cost," Sarah added, "but we think it's important to make a contribution."

"Oh, I think that's wonderful," Holly said, a huge smile lighting up her face. She clasped her hands together and placed them in her lap. "Every bit helps. And just think, when the steeple is finally finished, this entire community can take pride that we all chipped in toward the restoration."

Pastor Blake clapped enthusiastically, grinning from ear to ear, a huge smile that rivaled the one plastered on Holly's face. Dylan felt a sudden yearning. The fellowship and community he was witnessing within the walls of Main Street Church left him awestruck. Never in his life had he experienced something so profound. As he gazed upon Holly, her face radiant with joy, he felt the stirrings of something so powerful inside him it caused a painful tightening in his chest. Rooted to the spot, he didn't think he could take his eyes off Holly if his life depended on it. A longing swept through him, pure and deep, and although he didn't fully understand the scope of it, he knew that he wanted to be a part of this community, this wonderful landscape. This little oasis from the storms of life.

Every day he was finding new things to appreciate about life in West Falls. The warm, down-to-earth townsfolk. Doc, his wise landlord. Pastor Blake and Main Street Church. Horseshoe Bend Ranch and all its many opportunities. And above all else, Holly. In many ways she was everything he'd always wanted in a woman—kind, beautiful, spiritual, funny.

But as much as he was beginning to enjoy life in West Falls and his budding relationship with Holly, he couldn't run the risk of getting involved with her and then finding himself in a situation that was over his head. Not when he was filled with so much uncertainty. Not when the chances of hurting her were so great if things didn't work out. The life she led wasn't easy by any means. Every day presented new challenges and on-going struggles. And if he was being completely honest with himself, the ramifications of his new life scared him to death.

Chapter Six

Dylan gently held the colt's hoof in his hand, his attention focused on the small stone stuck in the heel. With all the precision he possessed, he extracted the stone, soothing the horse afterward by patting him on his side. He sure was a looker, Dylan noted. The spirited colt had been limping for a few days, a fact that was causing great worry to Holly, according to Malachi. Thankfully, he was none the worse for wear.

"Good boy, Picasso," he crooned. "You're a real champ. I know it must have hurt to have me poking around, but you handled it like a trooper." The colt let out a nicker in response, giving Dylan a reason to chuckle.

"Keep that up and you're going to make yourself indispensable around here." The low timbre of Malachi's voice slid into the silence of the stables. "You saved me a call to Shep, our local vet."

Dylan wasn't surprised by his presence. He'd known the minute Malachi entered the stables, despite his attempts to be unobtrusive. It was a skill he'd learned in

Afghanistan. Being aware of your surroundings had been a matter of life and death in a combat zone.

From what he was discovering about the ranch foreman, he was a keen observer of all things and a lot more talkative than he'd appeared the first day they'd met.

Dylan swiped his arm across his forehead. "The good news is it was only a stone. The way he was limping around the corral, I thought he might have a puncture wound that developed into an abscess. Or possibly a case of thrush."

"That's something to be thankful for. This colt means an awful lot to Holly and Tate. Cassidy, too."

"I figured as much. From what Holly told me about the night of his birth, Picasso is a little superstar around here."

"He came into the world with a real bang, that's for sure." Malachi seemed to be studying him as if he was trying to read his mind. "Dylan, there's something I'd like to talk to you about."

Dylan stood up and faced him, giving the other man his full attention.

"I have to leave the ranch for a bit. A week at the very least. My grandfather on the reservation isn't doing too well."

"I'm sorry to hear that," he said. "I'll remember to keep him in my prayers." Ever since the explosion he'd gotten real good at praying. For some reason, praying for others was more satisfying than asking for his own to be answered. Perhaps because ever since he was a kid he'd been praying for a lot of things that had never come to pass. And somehow, it made him feel more connected to the people around him to offer up prayers on their behalf. It made him feel like part of a community.

Pray for one another, that you shall be healed. The words of his hometown pastor rang in his ears, reminding him that there were certain things from childhood he'd held onto. Not everything had been bad. There were some things he proudly carried with him. Within him there were remnants of a childhood scattered with random acts of kindness and generosity. A pastor who'd taken him under his wing. A schoolteacher who'd encouraged him to reach for the stars. A mother who'd loved him unconditionally.

Malachi stood before him and scratched his chin, deep in thought. "Problem is, Holly depends on me for her riding lessons. I'd hate to slow down her momentum, since she's turned a corner."

"She's certainly making progress," Dylan said with a nod of his head. Over the past two weeks, he'd caught glimpses of Holly riding Sundance in the corral, aided by Malachi. She looked stronger and more in control. Her face no longer reflected fear. "Her confidence seems to be growing, and she's building up her endurance a bit."

"She's definitely stronger, although she tries to push herself past exhaustion at times. You said you worked with disabled riders back in Oklahoma, so it wouldn't be too much of a stretch for you to spot Holly while she's riding. Can you handle filling in for me?" The question hovered in the air between them. It was also the most words Malachi had uttered to him since he'd come on board several weeks ago.

Could he handle it? His initial reaction was to bris-

tle at the suggestion that he might not be able to. He'd
handled two tours of duty in Afghanistan, hadn't he?
It didn't get any tougher than that. Then, as Malachi's
question settled in, he began to wonder. Could he? On
one hand, he loved spending time with Holly. The emotional attachment he felt toward her was strong, ce-
mented by months and months of writing to one another
and reading her wonderful, lively letters. Even before
he'd shown up in West Falls, he had a keen sense of who
she was as a person. Kind. Warm. Spirited. A woman of
faith. Being in close contact with her would serve only
to tighten their bond, and he wasn't sure he wanted that
to happen. It would only make it harder to walk away
from her in a few months' time. And he did intend to
leave West Falls. Being in Holly's presence reminded
him way too much of the fragility of life. It made him
feel defenseless and vulnerable. He hated feeling that
way. Stepping in with a few words of advice while she
was riding Sundance was one thing. Driving her into
town so she could meet with the teen group had been
the right thing to do under the circumstances. Being
solely responsible for Holly's care and safety during
the lesson was something completely different. It made
him responsible for her.

There was no way he was going to admit it to Malachi, but the very thought of it terrified him. *What if
something happens? What if I don't know how to care
for her needs?* Just the idea of it made him feel uneasy.
It put him way too close to that dark space he'd been
trapped in, that netherworld of fear and doubt. It served
as a constant reminder of what he might have lost if
he hadn't regained the use of his legs. It forced him to

face his worst fear head-on. What was he thinking to even consider it?

He swallowed past the huge lump in his throat. "Isn't there anybody else?"

Malachi shook his head. "Holly's parents would step in if they were here, but they won't be back from their horse auction trip for a few more days." Malachi was staring at him, barely blinking as he waited for an answer. "How about it?"

"I'd rather not," he said in a no-nonsense, clipped tone. He reached up and fidgeted with the collar of his T-shirt as heat suffused his face.

Malachi frowned, his onyx-colored eyes widening in surprise. "Why?" he said, seeming to lose his composure a little bit. He'd never heard such consternation in Malachi's voice. "What's the problem?" Malachi pressed.

Why? There were dozens of answers to that question, none of which he wanted to share with Malachi. The idea of getting so near Holly was nerve-racking. The thought of getting pulled in any deeper than he already was sent waves of uncertainty crashing over him. Without knowing it, Malachi was putting him in a corner by asking him to fill in during his absence. He was pushing his buttons.

"Why?" he snapped. "I'm just not comfortable doing it, that's all."

He heard the slight whirring sound just before Holly's voice sliced into the silence. "Don't worry about it, Malachi. At the moment I don't want a single thing from Dylan, least of all his help." With eyes blazing and a mutinous look stamped on her face, Holly wheeled herself around and barreled out the door, her blond hair flying around her like a whirlwind. There was no doubt in his mind that she was attempting to get as far away as possible from the very sight of him.

Heat crept up the back of her neck as she flew out of the stables and quickly made her way toward her van. The path in front of her was clouded by a red haze swirling around her. Hot, pulsing anger was flowing through her veins. She moved to get as far away from Dylan as her chair would take her.

"Arrogant, selfish jerk," she muttered. "As if the world revolves around him!"

The crunching noise of cowboy boots rang out in the stillness of the afternoon.

"Holly, wait up! Please." The sound of Dylan's voice grated in her ears like nails on a chalkboard. She didn't even bother turning around. There was nothing he could say at the moment that she wanted to hear. She couldn't recall a moment in recent memory when she'd been so disappointed in a person.

All of sudden Dylan planted himself in front of her, causing her to almost crash into him. She gritted her teeth, scowling up at him. "Get out of my way before I run you over!" she growled. "I mean it."

He leaned over till they were eye level, firmly placing his hands on the chair arms to stop her from moving away from him.

"Please give me a chance to explain," Dylan said. His features were strained, his mouth creased with tension. Steely determination shone from his eyes. He pushed up his cowboy hat so she was able to see his eyes.

She shook her head, feeling mutinous. "I heard what you said. You made it sound as if Malachi asked you to babysit me! And you made it crystal clear that you don't intend to help me with my lessons. As far as I can see, there's really nothing to explain."

His mouth quirked. Green eyes bore into hers so intently she wrapped her arms around her middle in a protective gesture. There was no way she was going to let him hurt her any further. As it was, she found herself with a racing pulse and abnormal breathing. She couldn't remember the last time she'd been so fired up about something. Or someone.

"I'm sorry if I sounded callous back there. It wasn't my intention." His tone softened to the point of gentleness. "When Malachi asked me about the riding lessons, I felt put on the spot. I'll admit it. I felt a little boxed in."

Her chest was rising and falling sharply. She felt her nostrils flaring as her temper spiked. "Boxed in? Did you seriously just say that?" She rolled her eyes. "Wherever did you get that silver tongue of yours?"

Dylan let out a wild groan. His expression was sheepish. "I just keep putting my foot in my mouth, don't I?" He stood up, pacing back and forth in front of her, his fingers idly toying with the brim of his cowboy hat. "Truth is, the idea of being responsible for your welfare during the lesson rattles me." He threw his hands up and let out a huff of air. "There! I said it out loud. I'm afraid that I won't know what I'm doing—that I'll hurt you. And the thought of hurting you tears me up inside." The vulnerability in his voice touched a tender part of her. Against her will, she found her anger dissipating. He was afraid? This strong, fierce soldier was nervous about hurting her? In a way, it made sense. Hadn't it taken her a while to get comfortable in her own skin after the accident? Hadn't she been a bit overwhelmed by the enormity of her challenges? How could she expect him to feel any differently? This was all new to him.

"Everything could have been avoided if you'd just been straight with Malachi." She frowned at him, annoyed at his ability to worm his way back into her good graces so rapidly. Why did he have so much power over her emotions?

"I'm only here for a short stint, Holly. The more time we spend together—" He seemed to be searching wildly for the right words. "I don't want to complicate your life."

She snorted. "My life? Or yours?"

He wrinkled his forehead, his handsome face looking perplexed. "What do you mean by that?"

"Ever since you arrived in West Falls, you've been tiptoeing around me, pretending that you didn't come here to start a relationship with me. Avoiding the elephant in the room." She slapped her palms against her legs. "Well! It's right here. My legs. My disability. The reason you can't possibly think of me in the same way as you did before you met me in person."

Tension crackled in the air between them. Their gazes were locked on each other, neither one blinking. She spotted a muscle twitching over his eyelid, saw the stress in his clenched jaw. He seemed to be breathing out of his nose.

"Holly, I'd be lying if I said nothing's changed between us. I know you had your reasons, but you hid a very essential truth about yourself from me. That in itself changed our relationship, because you didn't trust me enough to be straight with me. You didn't give me a chance to make up my own mind about whether or not it was something I could handle. For someone who's been lied to ever since he was a child, that's a lot to swallow." He brushed his hand across his face, appearing worn out. "But there's plenty of things that have stayed the same. When I'm around you, I still feel as if I've known you my whole life. I get that easy, laid-back feeling that doesn't come around very often. At least not for me. I still care about you. Very much."

She swallowed, overwhelmed by Dylan's heartfelt words. She felt the same way. From the very beginning she'd known their friendship was special, a once-in-a-lifetime connection. And she'd been hoping for more. Much, much more. But she couldn't put those feelings into words because she didn't want to put Dylan in any more of an awkward position than he was already in. Truth be told, she didn't want to deal with rejection. And he'd referenced being deceived ever since childhood, something she couldn't even fathom. His words spoke of deep layers of pain.

"And by the way, you're wrong about something," he continued. "Thinking about you is all I've done for the past year. Thinking. Dreaming. Wanting. Hoping. And it hasn't changed all that much, even though I've tried my best to get you out of my mind."

She wet her lips, eager to know why he was trying to rid her from his thoughts. "Why are you trying so hard?" she asked in a raspy voice.

He reached down and touched her cheek with his

fingers, slowly trailing them down to the side of her neck. His tenderness caused her to tremble. "You want to know why? Since you're tired of me tiptoeing around, here goes. I've been running away from things for most of my life. When things get tough or too hot to handle, I shut down. I leave." He closed his eyes for a second. "I'm not proud of it, but it's true. What kind of man would I be if I started something with you that I wasn't sure I could finish?"

Confusion flooded her. Was he trying to say he was sparing her from being hurt down the road? Or that he was scared? She didn't know what to make of either scenario.

"I don't know, Dylan. Maybe you should ask yourself what's worse—not being able to finish something or not even having the gumption to try."

Before Dylan could respond, she made her way to her van, not even bothering to glance back at him before she lifted herself up and into the center console, then reached down to pull her manual wheelchair in behind her. In a matter of minutes she roared off, leaving Dylan in her wake.

Chapter Seven

Ever since leaving Dylan the previous day at the stables, Holly hadn't been able to stop herself from replaying their encounter in her mind. It didn't sit well with her that things were so up in the air between them. Rather than sit around at home and fret over the situation, she was headed to lunch with the roses. If that didn't get her mind off Dylan, she didn't know what would.

As Holly wheeled herself up the ramp entrance to the Falls Diner, a thrill of anticipation fluttered in her chest. As she swung the door open, the smell of downhome cooking assailed her senses, causing her belly to rumble with appreciation. A strong sense of nostalgia swept over her. Robin, a waitress at the diner and Doc Sampson's granddaughter, greeted her with a friendly smile before ushering her to her regular table. As she made her way down the aisle, she spotted the girls at the table chatting animatedly amongst themselves. They were sitting at the booth next to the neon-colored jukebox. It had always been their favorite, the one they'd sat in when they were in high school.

The four roses—Holly, Cassidy, Jenna and Regina. The nickname had been attached to them since their teen years. Best friends since childhood, they'd been inseparable throughout their youth. When they were in high school, Doc had laughingly declared this particular table as the roses' table, due to their frequent visits. And they'd seized every opportunity to sit there, like princesses on a throne. The diner had been the local hangout for the teenagers in West Falls, and the four of them had been regular customers. Doc's best customers, if she remembered correctly. This place held a lot of great memories. As a matter of fact, she'd had her first date here. At the time she'd been crazy about Bobby Simons. For a while there, they'd been the "it" couple of the senior class, until he'd broken things off after the accident. Although she'd been crushed by his abrupt decision, she'd soon realized the wisdom in ending things. At eighteen years old, he hadn't wanted to be saddled with a young woman recovering from traumatic injuries. After being dumped by Bobby, she'd guarded her heart against any man she thought might break it. Until now. Until Dylan had entered her life with his inspiring, wonderful letters.

After putting the brake on her wheelchair, she placed her purse on the table. Using her arms, she raised herself up and swung her legs over so she was seated in the booth next to Cassidy. Since she was a regular customer, Robin knew the drill. The waitress pushed the wheelchair to the back of the restaurant, where she would fold it up and park it in the coatroom.

Holly looked around the table at the three roses, the best friends any girl would be blessed to have in their lives. They all greeted her warmly, their faces lit up with smiles. There was such comfort in knowing their weekly routine of having lunch together was still going strong after four months. In many ways it was the highlight of her week, especially since their ties had been severed for so many years. It was fun catching up and falling into their old, familiar rhythms. The laughter they shared was good for the soul.

"Four volcano cheeseburgers with curly fries. Am I right?" Robin asked upon returning to the table.

They all nodded their heads. It was their standard order, just as it had been back in high school. A warmth settled in her chest at the knowledge that some things never changed. It was a comforting thought in an ever-changing world.

Robin twirled a finger through her pink, shoulder-length hair. "And four chocolate shakes?"

"Yep. Might as well go all out," Jenna declared, patting her nonexistent belly.

"Make mine strawberry," Regina corrected. "I'm living on the edge today."

The girls all burst into laughter at the notion of Regina taking a walk on the wild side with a strawberry shake. Jenna laughed harder than anyone, a fact Holly found hard to ignore. With her long dark hair, caramel-hued eyes and exotic coloring, Jenna was stunning. And for more years than she'd like to count, her friend had been standoffish, staying as far away from the West Falls community as possible. Getting Jenna back into the fold had been a gradual process over the past few months. Even though she still remained a bit reserved, she seemed genuinely happy to be spending time with them. Because of her deep love for animals, she'd even started working as an assistant with Shep, the local veterinarian.

All four of the roses had been forced to realize that the car accident had torpedoed their friendships, turning best friends into distant strangers. When Cassidy had returned to West Falls last spring, old secrets had been revealed, creating a healing balm for all of them. They'd vowed never to let their connections be severed again and to accept responsibility for the accident as a foursome. The townsfolk were still grappling with the revelation that the accident had been the result of horseplay. At first, Jenna had been opposed to revealing their secret, insisting that they'd all promised to uphold their vow to one another. In the end, truth won out, and the four roses were now dealing with the fallout as best they could. They were still in the process of rebuilding their once-unbreakable bond and moving forward with their lives.

Cassidy picked up a spoon and rattled it against her glass. "Ladies, I have an announcement to make." Once she had their full attention, Cassidy continued, "I wanted to let you know that Tate and I have set a date for the wedding. It's December 10." Jenna, Regina and Holly began to hoot and holler, causing Cassidy to raise her hands to cover her ears because of the commotion. A few customers at neighboring tables swiveled around and regarded them with curiosity.

"So," Cassidy continued, "I would like to formally ask the three of you to be my bridesmaids." A momentary hush fell over the table.

"Oh, Cassidy, I'd be honored," Holly said, breaking the silence. She was over the moon for the couple. Words couldn't express the joy she felt in having her best friend become her sister-in-law. After all these years, it was finally coming to fruition.

"I wouldn't miss the chance to be part of this town's wedding of the year," Regina added. She was beaming at her cousin. It was nice to see, Holly thought, considering there had always been a slight rivalry between the two. Regina had always felt second best to Cassidy, and for many years, she'd felt as if she'd stood in her cousin's shadow. Being the daughter of two self-absorbed, neglectful parents had left Regina with a lot of baggage. Most times she hid it behind a veneer, but Holly knew the pain was still there, resting under the surface.

Jenna sat across the table, biting her lip and twiddling her fingers. "Are you sure you'd like me to be in the wedding?" she asked in a tentative voice.

Cassidy reached out and clasped Jenna's hand in her own. "Of course I am, Jenna. I wouldn't have it any other way. Now that we're all back in each other's lives, I'm hoping we can get back to that place in time where we could finish each other's sentences."

Jenna let out a relieved breath and smoothed back her long dark hair. "Thanks for asking me to be part of your and Tate's special day. It means a lot."

"It will be fun to wear a formal gown and get a little fancy," Holly said with a grin. "A nice change of pace for me."

Regina shook her head as she pointed in Holly's direction. "Yes, it will. I can't believe you're still wearing those T-shirts."

Holly frowned as she looked down at her You Rock, I Roll T-shirt. "What's wrong with it?"

"The shirts are cute—" Regina seemed to be struggling for the right words.

Holly crinkled her nose. "But?"

Regina, Cassidy and Jenna exchanged looks.

Cassidy spoke in a gentle, supportive tone. "You could mix it up a bit. Blues and pinks are great with your coloring."

"Hey!" Holly protested. "I got all dolled up for the benefit for Main Street Church, didn't I?"

"You sure did. And you looked amazing," Regina gushed.

She racked her brain for more evidence that she wasn't a walking fashion disaster. "And I wear a nice outfit every time I do my speaking engagements."

"Ease up, girls. If she's happy with herself, she shouldn't have to change who she is," Jenna insisted.

Cassidy pressed on. "Are those T-shirts who you are, Holly? Or simply your way of telling the world you've accepted your situation and you can be irreverent about it?"

Cassidy's question caused her to stop and think for a moment. At first the T-shirts had been a statement to the world, her way of saying, "Yes, I'm paralyzed. I'm in a wheelchair. I've accepted it. Let's move on." She'd gotten used to wearing them, almost like a protective covering. Now that the roses mentioned it, she couldn't remember the last time she'd opted for anything other than a T-shirt. She hadn't even realized how far she'd taken it.

She bit her lip. "I guess I have been hiding behind

them." She let out a ragged sigh. "Why go to all the effort when my dating prospects have been slim to none?"

Regina leaned forward across the table. "So what's going on between you and your soldier? Cassidy said he was hired on at the ranch."

"We're just friends, Regina. It's not romantic," she quickly answered. "And yes, he'll be working at the ranch for a few months." She bit her lip as she contemplated laying it all on the table. The four roses had made a deal to be honest with one another about the goings-on in their lives. There was no time like the present.

"He didn't know until he showed up here that I was in a wheelchair."

Regina's eyes bulged. Jenna let out a little squeak. Cassidy reached out and put her arm around her.

"You never told him about the accident in any of the letters you exchanged?" a wide-eyed Jenna asked.

Regina eyed her with curiosity. "Not even a hint?"

Holly shook her head. There was no point in being embarrassed about it now. She couldn't go back in time and change things, despite how fervently she wished it were possible. All she could do was learn from her mistake. And try to understand why she'd lacked the courage to be completely transparent to Dylan. Why hadn't she felt as if she were enough?

"No, I didn't tell him. For some reason even I don't fully understand, I couldn't. I'm more ashamed of that than anything I've ever done since the accident." She wet her lips, determined to confide in the roses. "I got so caught up in Dylan. I guess I just didn't want him to view me any differently."

Jenna squeezed her hand. "You're allowed to make mistakes. Don't beat yourself up about it."

Regina's gaze was focused somewhere in the distance. Clearly, she hadn't even been listening to her moment of introspection.

"Sorry to go off topic, but who's that tall drink of water standing at the counter? There should be a law against someone being that good-looking."

A frisson of awareness rippled through her. In a small town like West Falls, there weren't too many strangers who would fit that description. Holly glanced over her shoulder only to clap eyes on Dylan as he stood at the counter, chatting up Doc. He wore a light brown cowboy hat on his head, a white cotton T-shirt and a pair of well-worn jeans. His muscles were on full display. She quickly turned back toward the table, not wanting him to feel obligated to come over, especially after their dust-up the previous day. This was the first time she'd seen him since then, and it was bound to be awkward for both of them. As she'd made it clear to Dylan, obligation was the last thing she wanted from him.

"That's him…Dylan," she explained to the girls, her voice sounding way calmer than she felt on the inside. In response, Regina let out a low whistle. Her friend's enthusiasm made Holly smile.

There was no denying Dylan's masculine appeal. The short dark hair paired with the startling green eyes. His chiseled features. His rugged, manly build. She imagined his good looks garnered a lot of female attention wherever he went. She stuffed down the twinge of jealousy she felt at the idea of Dylan being sought after by the female population in West Falls. After all, it wasn't as if she had any claim on him. He was as free as a bird.

"He is handsome, isn't he?" she asked the roses. All three women nodded their heads at Holly, echoing her sentiment. She felt her pulse quicken at the thought of Dylan being in such close proximity. Although she was trying to play it cool, she felt a huge grin overtaking her face.

"He's coming this way," Regina announced, her voice laced with excitement.

Holly felt a stab of uncertainty in her midsection. This might not be the most pleasant encounter in light of the fiery words they'd exchanged yesterday at the stables. There hadn't been an opportunity to clear the air, and it wouldn't have surprised her a single bit if he tried to avoid her. Seconds later she heard the clicking sound of cowboy boots on the parquet floor, right before she felt a tall, solid presence looming beside her. Holly tilted up her head, her pulse pounding as she met his gaze head-on. His brilliant green eyes glittered with an emotion she couldn't quite decipher. Dylan took off his cowboy hat and held it against his chest. He ran a hand through his rumpled hair.

"Afternoon, Holly," he said with a nod. His husky voice sent goose bumps racing up her arms. He scanned the faces around the table and nodded his head in greeting as he murmured, "Ladies. Nice to see you."

"Dylan, these are my friends, Jenna and Regina. You've already met Cassidy." Dylan's expression as he locked gazes with Cassidy could only be described as guarded. Turning toward Holly, he held up a to-go bag. With a sheepish grin that showcased his dimples he said, "These curly fries are addictive. This is my third order this week."

The knot in her stomach slowly began to ease up. Their spat seemed to be forgotten. "You're preaching to the choir. We've been eating them for most of our lives."

"Would you care to join us? We can pull up a seat," Regina offered.

"No, I've got to head back to the ranch. But thanks for asking." He shifted from one foot to the other. "Holly, I've got some free time this afternoon if you'd like a riding lesson."

She fidgeted uncomfortably in the booth. "A-are you sure? I wouldn't want to put you out."

"The only thing that would put me out is if you didn't accept my offer," he said smoothly, an expectant expression on his face. "It would be my pleasure."

"Well, then, I accept," she said, trying not to give in to the wild impulse to wrap her arms around his neck and place a grateful kiss on his cheek. He was instantly forgiven for being ornery yesterday. Words couldn't express how desperate she was to get back in the saddle. This unexpected offer from Dylan filled her with joy.

A smile tugged at the corners of his mouth. His handsome face held a relieved expression. "Well, then, I'll see you at two o'clock or so." He placed his cowboy hat back on his head and drawled, "Nice to meet you, roses."

After saying their goodbyes, silence reigned at the table until it was clear Dylan was out of earshot.

"Be still my heart," Regina murmured as she fanned herself with her hand.

Cassidy turned to Holly and raised her eyebrow. "I thought you said the two of you were just friends?"

"We are," Holly insisted, resisting the impulse to turn around and catch a last glimpse of Dylan as he exited the diner. She knew if she did the roses would never let her live it down.

Jenna playfully rolled her eyes. "Friends, huh? Is that why your face is lit up like a Christmas tree?"

Regina sent Holly an all-knowing look. "He's crazy about you. I can tell."

Holly felt her cheeks reddening. "No, he's not."

"She's right. He couldn't take his eyes off you," Jenna added. "Just be sure he's someone you can trust." She blurted out the words almost against her will. A shadow crossed her face and she broke eye contact, suddenly immersing herself in the contents of her plate.

Although Holly appreciated the subtle warning from Jenna, she sensed her friend was coming from a place of hurt. She couldn't put her finger on it, and Jenna had never revealed a single thing to confirm her suspicions, but she firmly believed something had happened to wound her soul. Something life changing.

Not for the first time, she prayed Jenna would find healing.

With regards to Dylan, she knew she could trust him. He was a good man, a strong and courageous soldier who'd devoted himself to keeping America out of harm's way. And he was a forgiving person. If not, he would have left West Falls as soon as he discovered her closely guarded secret. He'd never given her even the slightest reason not to have faith in him.

This was all foreign territory for her, Holly realized.

It had been ages since she'd sat with the roses and talked about boys and tender feelings. There hadn't been any romantic prospects in her life for eight long years. And although Dylan was a far cry from a boy, she still had nervous flutters in her stomach when it came to him, the same ones she'd dealt with as a teenager with her first crush. In the aftermath of the accident she'd been so focused on getting her bearings that she'd put romance on the back burner. Although it was a heady feeling to be the center of attention because a handsome cowboy paid attention to you, she was determined not to get carried away. Doing so had already caused a big mess and created friction between herself and Dylan. Besides, he wasn't interested in anything more complicated than friendship. He'd told her as much the other day.

"We had a pretty intense connection over the past year, but I could tell when we met in person he was uncomfortable with my being in a wheelchair. It was written all over his face," she confessed.

"Holly! That's not fair," Cassidy protested, her emerald eyes flashing with indignation. "He was taken by surprise, that's all. Anyone would have felt uncomfortable under the circumstances."

"I suppose you're right, Cass. I have to own that," she admitted, shrugging her shoulders.

"None of it matters anyway. He's only here for a short time, until his lease with Doc runs out."

"That's what I said when I came back to West Falls," Cassidy said drily. The roses laughed as she wiggled her engagement ring at them.

Yes, indeed. Cassidy had gotten her happily ever after with Tate. And she was now a permanent fixture in West Falls, even though she'd only planned on staying for the summer to care for her ill mother. *But you're not Cassidy,* a little voice whispered. *All you shared with Dylan were poignant letters exchanged during a period in his life when he was in a war zone and seeking normalcy. It wasn't real life!*

Perhaps their connection wasn't as strong as she'd hoped. In her fantasies she'd imagined a glorious future for the two of them, filled with a courtship, a wedding and a white picket fence. No, she wasn't going to wrap her head around those pipe dreams. She just couldn't. Allowing herself to hope for something to blossom between her and Dylan was asking for trouble. And a world of hurt. Because, regardless of what the roses seemed to think, she couldn't shake the feeling that when Dylan looked at her he couldn't see past her lie of omission about being in a wheelchair and the complications it presented.

Two hours later Dylan had saddled up Sundance and assisted Holly in the process of mounting her horse. It surprised him how smoothly things were going. With the ramp, Holly was able to mount Sundance at the top of the platform where her wheelchair was level with the horse. His assistance was primarily making sure the horse was steady, lifting her up by the waist and helping her get situated on Sundance. Her upper-body strength showcased amazing power. Despite the fear gnawing at him, everything was working out just fine. Way better than he'd imagined.

As he'd discussed with Malachi, Holly's skills were rapidly improving, fueled by an increase in her endurance and a boost in confidence. After an hour's worth of riding, he could see the fatigue etched on Holly's face. Even though she didn't want to stop the lesson, he knew she'd reached her limit. Pushing her past it wasn't a good idea. Malachi had warned him about such a scenario. Against her wishes, he put an end to the session, earning himself a gigantic smile by promising to give her another one tomorrow. Once he'd helped Holly dismount and get back in her chair, she wheeled herself toward the stables, coming back out in a matter of minutes with a picnic basket and a blanket in her lap. She smiled at him mischievously.

"I think we've earned a little break," she said, holding out the blanket to him. He looked around him for the perfect place to set up, noticing a small tree a few feet away from the stables. When he reached the spot, he began spreading out the black-and-red checkered blanket, appreciative of the shade the tree provided. Holly was right behind him, the picnic basket in her hands. After taking it from her, Dylan watched as Holly put the brake on her chair, then lowered herself down onto the blanket. He settled himself beside her, marveling at her quiet strength and independence.

Barely able to contain his curiosity, Dylan asked, "So what's in the basket?"

"It's a peace offering of sorts." Holly looked him straight in the eye, her face full of contrition. "I had no business blowing up at you the other day."

"Are you kidding me? You had every right to blow off some steam. It makes me cringe just thinking how I must have sounded." He made a clucking sound with his teeth. "I know you must have been calling me all kinds of a fool."

"Were your ears burning?" she asked, sending him a mischievous look.

Holly flipped the lid of the picnic basket and pulled out two napkins and two bottles of water, then reached in again and pulled out two mouthwatering cupcakes. She placed one in front of him on the napkin.

"Are these carrot cakes?" The sight of the sweet treat had him practically salivating. A low rumble began emanating from his stomach, causing Holly to laugh.

"Yes, they are. I remember you writing in one of your letters how you couldn't wait to get one of your mother's carrot cakes." She held up her hands. "Doc deserves the credit, though. I bought them at the diner."

"She made me a batch for my homecoming ceremony." He reached out and picked up one from his napkin, letting out a sound of satisfaction as the rich taste hit his tongue. "Mmm. They've always been my favorite." He put a finger to his lips. "Just don't tell my mama, but these are almost as good."

Amusement flickered in Holly's eyes. "I'm glad you're enjoying them."

Gratitude swelled inside him for Holly's thoughtful gesture. More and more he was seeing the complete picture of Holly and who she was as a person based on her unselfish actions and sweet nature. Caring. Giving. Grateful. Ever faithful.

"You didn't have to do this, Holly."

"Are you kidding me? You've gone above and beyond with the riding lessons. The least I could do is feed you."

"I'm grateful for it, but you don't have to be beholden to me. I'm an employee here."

Holly visibly stiffened and stopped nibbling her cupcake, midbite. Her eyes held a wounded expression. Within seconds she'd masked her countenance, no longer appearing stricken.

"I didn't mean—" He fumbled with his words. "That's not the only reason I helped out today. You're my friend, Holly. I enjoy spending time with you."

Friends? Who was he trying to kid? They were clearly more than friends, although he didn't know how to categorize her. On some level, both of them knew he hadn't come all the way to Texas for friendship. Even though things were more complicated than he'd imagined before coming to town, he still felt much more than friendship for her. Denying it wouldn't change a thing. It was still there, resting against his heart. And it was growing stronger each and every day.

"I've never felt as close to someone as I do to you," he blurted. "And I've never properly thanked you for writing me. Your letters meant the world to me. In fact, hearing all about your life in West Falls opened up a whole new world for me. Hearing about this ranch kept me sane. It helped me stay strong in moments when I thought I couldn't last another day over there. So thank you, Holly Lynch."

She sent a pearly grin in his direction. "You don't have to thank me. I got as much from your letters as I gave to you. Your stories about military life made me want to be brave, even when I didn't particularly feel like it."

Dylan frowned. "Something tells me you didn't need

me to give you courage. You're pretty humble about your recovery, but Doc told me all about the accident and how you endured. You persevered, Holly. And now you're thriving. That makes you a very strong woman."

"I've always had my family by my side, as well as the doctors. They make the world of difference."

The world of difference. He'd felt the same way when his mother had flown to his side at the military hospital and willed him back to good health with equal doses of prayer, love and devotion.

"I know what you mean," he admitted. "Mama did the same for me. She'd never even been on a plane before, but she flew all the way overseas to be with me. She pretty much used all her life savings to fly to the hospital and stay with me during my recovery." His throat clogged, and tears pricked at his eyes. The memory of her dedication never failed to move him. "She was my lifeline."

Holly reached out and clasped his hand, giving it a comforting squeeze. "From everything you wrote to me about her, she sounds like a good woman and an even greater mom."

He nodded, not even trusting himself to speak at the moment. His emotions were too close to the surface, too raw. For so long, it had been the two of them against the world, fighting all the battles together as a united front. She'd never let him down. Not one single time. She'd never missed any of his baseball games, and she'd sat in the bleachers and cheered for him at his high school graduation. He was overjoyed that she'd finally found a man worthy of her love and affection, even though her new life had led her to New Mexico.

"My mother and I are going through a rough patch at the moment," Holly said, her eyes swirling with emotion. "She kept some information from me that I had every right to know. Things have been strained between us for the past few months."

Dylan frowned. "I don't mean to pry, but is it something that can be mended?" He knew all too well about fractured family dynamics.

Holly shook her head, her expression muted. "I'm praying on it. Dad called me the other night. My parents will be back in a few days from their horse-scouting trip, so it might be a good time to try to mend some fences."

"I'm sure she'll meet you halfway," Dylan said, a smile tugging at the corners of his mouth. "From what you've told me about your family, there's a lot of love and devotion there."

"Dylan, if you don't mind my asking, what about your father? In all your letters, you never once mentioned him."

For a moment he hesitated. He felt his back tensing up. His hands tightened into fists. The topic of his father was a prickly one. There were still so many unresolved issues between them, so much animosity and bitterness. It was embarrassing to admit to this amazing woman that his father had never wanted him. He'd been cast off.

Clearing his throat, he said, "Basically, I didn't have a father. Not one to speak of anyway. He bailed on me and Mama before I was even born."

"I'm so sorry," Holly said in a mournful voice. "That must have been difficult."

He shrugged, not wanting Holly to pity him. "He and my mother loved each other at one point. Or so she says. They grew up together in Madden, even though she came from a rougher side of town. My mom says they were high school sweethearts. So when she found herself pregnant, he proposed." He let out a ragged sigh. "They never made it down the aisle, though."

Holly's blue eyes shone with surprise. "No? What happened?"

"When the daughter of the richest man in town took a fancy to him, my so-called father took off in a flash." He fiddled with his collar as heat suffused his neck. It was tough to admit his father was a man of such dubious morals. "I guess he saw a better deal with her."

She nibbled at her nail, then shoved her fingers under her legs so she wouldn't be tempted to bite them. "Did he end up marrying the other woman?"

Yes." He spit the word out as if it were poison. "And he had two perfect kids with her, all the while refusing to do right by me and my mama. He never acknowledged me as his kid, although everyone figured it out and we became the target of the town gossipmongers. Every now and then he would throw me a bone and take me to a baseball game or the circus. It was usually in the next town over where no one would see us."

He fought past the lump in his throat. It was painful to dredge up a lifetime of hurt and disappointment. He wondered if he'd be choking on it for the rest of his life.

She nodded, her eyes radiating compassion and understanding, even though he imagined Holly's childhood had been picture-perfect. How in the world could she relate to such a messed-up situation? She chewed on her lip. "How awful, Dylan!"

Awful. That didn't even begin to describe it. It had been pure torment. But living in Madden had taught him a lot about survival, lessons he'd taken right along with him to Afghanistan. He liked to think those early lessons had kept him alive in a war zone. They had made him sharper and stronger, with an ability to land on his feet no matter what was thrown at him.

His gaze locked with Holly's. There was so much emotion in their azure depths. Despite all she'd been through, things that might have hardened a person, she still had empathy for him. Her eyes said it all. She ached for all he'd endured.

But he still hadn't told her the extent of the injuries he'd sustained. He hadn't yet revealed his own devastating experience with losing the use of his legs. As difficult as his ordeal had been, it was nothing compared to all Holly suffered. And she still had day-to-day challenges. Guilt began to creep in on him.

"I hate to complain about it after all you've been through. It must have been terrifying to wake up in a hospital bed and have a doctor tell you about your paralysis."

Her mouth tightened. "It was actually my parents and Tate who delivered the news. They made sure to be the ones to tell me." The look on her face spoke of hardship and loss. "Even though it was devastating, learning about the gravity of the situation from my loved ones was a blessing. When I lost it, at least I had the three of them there to hold me as I fell apart."

"And your recovery. What was that like?" he prodded, overwhelmed by curiosity about her journey.

She winced. "It took months to learn how to roll over, get dressed by myself, feed myself. I had to learn all the things most able-bodied people take for granted. That's one of the reasons these lessons mean the world to me. Riding Sundance makes me feel like my old self. It helps me feel independent. I still have a lot of mountains to climb on this journey, but I'm determined to get there."

He felt something tighten in his chest and he knew that he couldn't hold out on her a minute longer. It wasn't fair to just sit here and listen while she bared her soul. He owed her so much more than that. Clumsily, he searched for the right words to say. "Do you remember what I wrote to you about the injuries I sustained two and a half years ago?"

Her eyes went wide. "Of course. The Humvee you were traveling in… It was attacked, wasn't it? That's when your friend Benji was killed."

Benji. He tried not to think of him too often. Benji, with his Southern twang and gentle demeanor. He'd told more knock-knock jokes than Dylan had even knew existed. Even when they'd been stinkers, he'd found himself laughing. There was something so genuine and good-hearted about him. Dylan had never met a soldier more proud of his origins. Benji didn't hesitate to boast about hailing from the finest town in Virginia. Manassas, Virginia. Benji told anyone who would listen about his hometown being the site of the First Battle of Bull Run in 1861. His friend's patriotism has come at a devastating price. He'd lost his life protecting the freedoms most people took for granted.

"Holly, what I want to tell you—" He put his cupcake down on his napkin and fiddled clumsily with his fingers. "What I need to let you know is that I can relate to your situation more than most. My injuries were quite serious. For a while there I was in really rough shape. I was out of commission for months."

Holly made a tutting sound. "That's tough. I know what it's like to be confined to a hospital bed and staring at four walls. It makes you value the normal, everyday life you lived before everything tilted on its axis and changed."

He sucked in a deep breath. "Holly, there's more. We have more in common than you know. The reason I was in the hospital for so long was because I lost the use of my legs, just like you did."

Chapter Eight

I lost the use of my legs, just like you did.

The words slammed into her with the force of an explosion. She grappled with Dylan's words, immediately assuming she'd misheard him.

"Wh-what do you mean?"

"My neck was broken as a result of the explosion. The force of the blast threw me from the Humvee. The doctors didn't think I would ever walk again. They told me as much when I woke up from a medically induced coma."

Broken neck. Legs. Coma. The details were whizzing around her like hummingbirds. But she couldn't seem to get past the shock induced by Dylan's announcement. Dylan had been paralyzed?

"How long? How long were you—?" She stumbled over the words, still reeling from his admission. So much of Dylan was reflected in his physicality. Being a soldier. His work around the ranch. Riding horses. For the life of her she couldn't imagine strong, powerful Dylan paralyzed.

"I couldn't walk for two months. Once the swelling on my spinal cord went down, I began doing physical therapy." Just reliving his experience seemed to have a drastic effect on Dylan. His complexion was ashen. Tight lines were drawn around his mouth and eyes. A look of stark terror flashed in his eyes.

"To be honest, the pain was excruciating. Fear was my biggest motivator. The thought of never walking again—" He stopped midsentence, appearing worried that he might have put his foot in his mouth again.

"It's okay to say it. You're being honest. For a while after the accident, I had this recurring dream where I regained the use of my legs." She let out a shaky laugh. "I grew to hate that dream, because as good as it felt while it was happening, there was a world of disappointment when I woke up and realized it wasn't true."

Silence stretched out between them. She was still grappling with this new information about Dylan. Her mind was working overtime trying to sort it all out when something clicked into place. Finding out the specifics of his injuries explained so much about Dylan and the way he viewed her.

She tilted her head toward him, eager to see his reaction to her question. "When you look at me, there's something else you see, isn't there?"

His brows shot up. "Something else? I'm not sure what you're talking about."

"I couldn't put my finger on it until this very moment, but I get it now. Every time you look at me it's as if you're reminded of your darkest hour, your worst fear. My being in a wheelchair really brings it all back for you, doesn't it? I'm the living, breathing embodiment of your nightmare, aren't I?"

Tears pricked at the back of her eyes, but she blinked them away. She could handle this, no matter what he had to say, no matter how badly it crushed her. It hurt so deeply to know that the very sight of her caused pain to Dylan. Because she cared for him. Deeply. And the sight of him did the very opposite to her. Her feelings were growing stronger and stronger every day. He was so much more now than the pen pal she'd reached out to as part of Main Street Church's ministry.

Dylan met her gaze without backing down. "Holly, you're right. When I first got to the ranch and realized you were paralyzed, the memories from the bomb blast came rushing back to me. They were like a tidal surge I couldn't hold back even if I tried."

His body shuddered. "I'm not sure I ever fully faced up to the events of that day. Losing Benji, having to deal with a devastating injury, feeling guilty about being alive when others weren't so fortunate. Being around you has helped me heal from all that. It's helped me face my fears. Seeing you working with the teens at Main Street Church and watching you tackle this riding thing head-on—" He shook his head. "It inspires me. I've been forced to take a good long look at myself and the things I haven't faced up to. More important, it's made me even more certain of what kind of man I want to be. I don't want to be the type of man who runs away when things get tough, even though I've done that a time or two in the past. I want to be more grounded in my faith so I don't feel so alone during the rough times."

"You never walk alone, Dylan. He's right beside you. Always."

"Thanks to you, I'm beginning to realize that, for the first time in my life. I'm so proud to know you, Holly Lynch."

She ducked her head down, overwhelmed by raw emotion and the beautiful sentiment he'd expressed. "I'm proud to know you, too, Dylan. In case I never told you in any of my letters, thank you for bravely serving this country. I know it wasn't easy."

Shivers went through her as she remembered some of the harrowing details from his letters. IEDs. Insurgents. Friends killed in the line of duty.

"It was my pleasure to serve and protect this country," he said with an easy grin, his adorable dimples on full display. "There are few things more important to me than family, good friends and this amazing country we call home."

Dylan reached out to her, clasping her smaller hand in the grip of his larger, roughened one. He leaned toward her, his shoulder brushing against hers as he swept a kiss across her forehead. As his lips moved over her skin, she pressed her eyes closed, cherishing this tender interlude, which she feared would pass all too soon.

This sweet moment of perfection, she thought, *will forever linger in my dreams.*

Sometime in the future—months and months after Dylan was gone for good—she could relive it over and over again. She wanted to take this moment and brand it on her soul so the feelings it evoked would never leave her. It would give her a sense of peace just knowing they'd shared something so special. As she opened her eyes she found Dylan gazing into them with a tenderness that left her breathless. They sat in companionable silence until Dylan made mention of getting back to work. They began packing up the empty water bottles and trash.

She said her goodbyes to Dylan, casting one lingering look over her shoulder as he ambled off toward the stables, his gait full of cowboy swagger. And even though she knew there were mountains standing between them, a small kernel of hope began to take flight within her soul. Could this really be happening? Was there a possibility of winning Dylan's heart before he left West Falls?

For the next week, Malachi stayed put at the reservation, during which time Dylan gave Holly almost daily lessons. He wasn't as nervous anymore about helping her out. So far, things had worked out well, although the past few times, she'd balked when he'd tried to end the lessons. At the moment, she was sitting on Sundance, her arms wrapped around her middle in a mutinous gesture.

"Dylan, I'm fine," she protested. "I could go another fifteen, twenty minutes."

"You don't want to wear yourself out," he said, trying to sound diplomatic. Although she was building up her endurance, he didn't want to push her too hard. As it was, she looked wiped out. He couldn't miss the signs—sweat gathered lightly on her forehead, winded breath, slumped posture. Her plucky personality made it impossible for her to say she'd had enough, even though she was dragging. Holly wanted so desperately to be back in the saddle and to make forward strides. She wouldn't hesitate to push past her limits in order to get there. As far as he was concerned, it wasn't happening. Not on his watch.

"Are you saying I look worn-out?" she huffed, placing a runaway curl back in place and wiping the sweat from her brow. At times he'd noticed her hair had a mind of its own, with the locks breaking free from the ponytail she'd placed it in. He liked seeing her hair falling all around her face. It softened some of her rough, tomboy edges. It made her look prettier than usual, if that were possible. As it was, she was stunning.

"Right now you're acting as stubborn as Rooster Cogburn."

Holly sputtered at the mention of her family's feisty rooster, a legendary character at the ranch. "Seriously? You're comparing me to a rooster?" Although her voice sounded indignant, Dylan could detect the amusement on her face and the twinkle in her eyes. She was seconds away from bursting into laughter.

"If the shoe fits," he drawled, intent on riling her up a little. "Come to think of it, your hair does get a little spiky from time to time."

She sputtered, her face resembling a storm cloud as she frowned at him. "One thing you better learn real fast about us Texas girls—never, ever insult our hair!"

Dylan threw back his head and laughed out loud. He couldn't remember the last time he'd had so much fun with someone. He liked the spirited side of Holly, even if it meant she was digging in her heels and acting ornery. Their easy banter made him feel almost weightless, and a happy feeling settled over him every time they went head-to-head. He'd never met anyone quite like her. He had the feeling if he searched the whole world over he'd never find another woman like Holly.

The sound of an approaching vehicle drew their attention away from their squabble and toward the dirt road situated just past the stables. The biggest horse trailer he'd ever seen came into view, then slowly made its way around the bends and stopped.

Holly let out a high-pitched squeal and began to fidget in the saddle. "Dylan, please help me down. My parents are here. They're back!"

As Dylan helped her down from Sundance, his mind began to whirl with the news. After several weeks on the road, the Lynches had finally returned from picking up their newly acquired horses. Holly had talked a blue streak about her parents during several of her riding lessons. From what he'd learned about them, they were exceptional people. Maggie Benson Lynch had grown up as the princess of Horseshoe Bend Ranch, with all the rights and privileges of being the daughter of a wealthy horse breeder. She'd been born with the proverbial silver spoon in her mouth. According to Holly it had been love at first sight when Frank Lynch had clapped eyes on Maggie.

"My dad was working at the ranch as a cowhand. My grandfather forbade the ranch hands from dating my mother, but once they laid eyes on each other... there wasn't a force on earth that could stop it." Clearly, Holly loved relaying the story. Her eyes had twinkled. Her skin had held a rosy glow.

"Your parents have built a beautiful life for themselves," he'd said, trying to keep a grip on his amazement. It was hard not to be impressed with all they'd achieved. Horseshoe Bend Ranch was a stunning monument to hard work and dedication.

"My grandfather, Lucas Benson, had a lot to do with it. He came to West Falls from Kentucky with barely a nickel to his name." Holly had shaken her head and chuckled.

"So how did your father win your grandpa's approval?" A cowhand winning the hand of the ranch owner's daughter? It sounded like a fairy tale to him.

"The old-fashioned way," Holly had answered, her voice tinged with pride. "He earned it by dedicating himself to this ranch and by making it his mission in life to generate more revenue and higher standards. And by chasing all the other boys away." She'd winked at him. "Gramps couldn't resist that."

Dylan shook himself out of his thoughts as two figures emerged from the cabin of the rig. He followed in Holly's wake as she quickly wheeled herself in their direction. A man he assumed to be her father strode toward her, meeting her halfway. As soon as he got within touching distance Holly wrapped her arms around his middle and hung on for dear life. He bent over and placed a kiss on the top of her head. Her mother walked over and ran her hands through Holly's hair, her gesture full of affection.

"If that hug was any indication, I dare say you missed us," Frank said as Holly released him from her grip.

"Maybe just a little bit," Holly teased, her voice breathless. "Mama. Daddy. I'd like you to meet Dylan Hart, a friend of mine. He's been hired on as a ranch hand and he's been giving me riding lessons, as well."

Dylan stuck his hand out to Mrs. Lynch. "I've heard an awful lot about the two of you. It's great to finally meet you."

"Nice to meet you, too, Dylan. Please call me Maggie. No one calls me Mrs. Lynch around here. It makes me feel ancient. And I don't do handshakes. Only hugs." Before he could comment, Maggie wrapped her arms around his shoulders and embraced him enthusiastically. Afterward, she stood back and grinned at him, her full cheeks resembling small plums.

Maggie Lynch was an attractive woman who exuded a vibe of ease and charm. With her expressive eyes and delicate features, she reminded him a bit of her daughter. The dark hair tinged with streaks of gray and the glasses perched on the bridge of her nose were uniquely her own. Frank Lynch was a bear of a man, well over six feet and broad shouldered. Frank reached out and clapped him on the shoulder, his twinkling blue eyes and warm smile immediately dispelling any doubts about his kindly nature.

"Welcome aboard, son. Any friend of my number one girl is always welcome at Horseshoe Bend Ranch," Frank said, his voice laced with enthusiasm.

Holly grinned at her father. "How was your trip home? You look a little tuckered out." Frank reached down and tugged lightly on a strand of Holly's hair. It was obvious that father and daughter shared a special bond. He didn't know if he was imagining it or not, but there seemed to be a slight tension between Holly and Maggie. Their interaction seemed a little strained.

"We made good time," Frank answered. "Every three to four hours we stopped to give the horses a water break. We spent last night in Houston, so the trip wasn't too bad. Wanted to make it home in time for the rodeo."

"The rodeo is not to be missed," Holly explained. "At least if you're a Lynch."

Maggie looked over at him. "One of the reasons we do our scouting in October is because of the temperature," Maggie explained. "The summer months are too brutally hot to safely transport horses any kind of distance. And we want to make sure all our horses are comfortable and healthy."

Frank chuckled. "In case you haven't guessed, this is more than a job for us. It's our life's passion. That and our two wonderful children."

Pride and an abundance of love rang out in Frank's voice as he spoke about Holly and Tate. Dylan felt a small stab of jealousy. What he wouldn't give to have a father who felt that way about him. To just once hear his father brag on him or hail his latest achievement would mean the world to him. Other than a few "atta boys" when he'd worked at the Bar M, there had been nothing to speak of. And he'd yearned for it. Like a starving person in search of a meal, he'd gone after any scrap of affection from him. Just when he'd felt as if they'd begun to establish a father-son bond, the rug had been pulled out from under him.

The memory of it still seared his insides. Because of it, he continued to harbor bitter feelings toward his father. It was like a festering sore that just wouldn't heal. And even though he was a fully grown adult, thinking about his father made him feel like that six-year-old boy who'd waited up half the night on Christmas Eve for his father to show up with his presents. Presents that hadn't made an appearance until a week later.

What kind of father will I be? Or husband? How can I give someone something that I never received? That I was never taught?

The questions roared through his mind like a freight train. He'd asked himself these things a hundred times or more. And even though he'd prayed on it, answers still eluded him. Finally, when he couldn't take it anymore, he glanced away from Holly and Frank, his throat clogged with a resentment that threatened to choke him.

"They're getting on like a house on fire, aren't they?" Her mother crept up on her while she was watching Dylan and her father standing side by side outside the trailer, talking and laughing as they sized up the horses.

"They seem to be," Holly answered, casting her mother a sideways glance. A little while ago her mother had gone up to the house and changed into a pair of dark-washed jeans and a long-sleeved shirt. Her father had been showing off the horses like a proud papa. She'd been content just watching Dylan's excitement over the animals.

Her mother reached down and tweaked her nose. "Penny for your thoughts. You seem to be miles and miles away from here."

"No, Mama. I'm right here." She let out a contented sigh. "I was just wishing this perfect moment could stretch out a little longer."

"Why? So you and your young man could canoodle as the sun goes down?" Maggie teased.

"He's not my young man," she said, a wistful tone echoing in her voice.

"Well, he could be if the two of you would only open your eyes and realize how right you are for one another."

"Mama! You've only just met Dylan. How on earth could you know that?" she scolded.

"You're so comfortable together. And you make such a handsome couple. With his dark head of hair and you being so fair, it's—"

"It's not that simple!" She cut her mother off. "Please, let's not pretend it's not a complicated issue. My life isn't easy. Doctor's appointments, daily medicine, doctor's bills, physical therapy."

"And everything you bring to the table counterbalances that—joy, laughter, support, faith."

She fought against a rising sense of annoyance. Why did her mother always try so hard to be her cheerleader? She didn't want anyone in her life to sugarcoat the situation with Dylan. That would only lead to disappointment and heartbreak. After everything she'd done to protect her daughter from hurt and rejection, surely her mother wouldn't want that.

Rebellion rose up inside her. Looking at things through rose-colored glasses wasn't going to do her any favors. "Dylan could be with anyone he wants! Look at him," Holly said, jutting her chin in his direction. No doubt at her father's insistence, Dylan had mounted one of the horses and was galloping around the arena, his every movement full of power and agility.

Her mother knitted her brows together. "And what if he wants to be with you? Is that so hard to fathom?"

Yes! she wanted to scream. *In a world full of able-*

bodied women, why would he ever choose me? Why would he choose a difficult road when he could easily take the path of least resistance? She didn't know why it was difficult to believe Dylan might have actual feelings for her. Why was it easier to believe she wasn't good enough to earn Dylan's love?

"Holly Lynch! Don't you dare look at me like that. You're good enough." Tears pooled in her mother's eyes and she choked out the words. "You're plenty good enough, baby girl." Without her even uttering a single word, her mother was able to read her like a book and tap into her innermost fears.

She glared at her mother, all her anger rising to the surface. "I'm not your baby girl, Mama. I haven't been for a very long time." Her voice bristled with things left unspoken. Tension crackled in the air between them. Her mother's face crumpled, and she let out a ragged sigh.

"Is there something you want to air out with me?" A heavy silence descended upon them. She tilted up her head, meeting her mother's gaze as she battled her bottled up emotions.

"Why did you do it? Why did you keep Cassidy's letters from me?" Her voice broke and she stifled a sob. After leaving West Falls eight years ago in the aftermath of the accident, Cassidy had written her dozens of letters, all of which her mother had intercepted in the mail and kept from her. It was only when Cassidy returned to town that her mother's actions had been uncovered. For months now, she'd avoided this confrontation, too frightened by the depth of her fury to deal with it head-on. She'd tamped down her feelings of betrayal, which had only made them fester.

"I can't believe I didn't come to you and admit what I'd done. Cassidy told me you knew someone kept her letters from you. By process of elimination, you must have guessed it was me."

Holly couldn't bring herself to speak. She simply nodded, acknowledging that she had indeed figured it all out. It was a painful discovery, but the facts had all pointed toward her mother.

"It's no excuse, but I suppose my shame was too great. Your whole life I've tried to teach you right from wrong and to walk a righteous path, yet I failed to do the same thing when I was presented with a choice. What I did—I could say it was done of out of love, but that wouldn't fully explain it. I was nervous and afraid—I was so angry at Cassidy for leaving after the accident. I blamed her for your injuries and for inflicting so much devastation. Not just on you but Tate, as well. He was heartbroken and humiliated when she broke off the engagement. And you were broken, in every possible way. When the letters started coming I told myself I would just tuck them away somewhere until you came home from the hospital. Until you were stronger. One day turned into another and another, until years had gone by…and the letters finally stopped coming."

"Were you ever going to tell me?" Her voice was raised, and it must have carried over to the driveway. Dylan glanced at them, his face creased with worry. She nodded in his direction, letting him know everything was fine. Or at least as fine as it could be under the circumstances.

"I like to think that I would have come clean eventually," her mother answered in a quiet voice. "I've learned from this, Holly. Forgiving Cassidy is the hardest thing I've ever done in my life. Gaining forgiveness from her for withholding those letters and keeping the two of you apart… It deeply humbles me. I can only pray you forgive me, as well."

She folded her hands in her lap. As much as she loved her mother, there was no way she could ignore all the resentment bubbling under the surface. And it wasn't just going to disappear because they'd aired things out. For eight long years she'd believed her best friend had turned her back on her. If her mother hadn't intercepted the letters, she could have been spared a world of pain. There was no way she could put into words what the loss of her best friend had done to her. Losing Cassidy had caused a physical ache in her soul that had never truly subsided until she came back to town.

She cast her eyes downward and cleared her throat. "I need time, Mama. Forgiveness isn't something I can just snap my fingers and give you. I wish it were that simple."

Her soul felt heavy as she forced the words out of her mouth. She wanted to be merciful, but she still ached for all those lost years between her and Cassidy.

When she looked up, the tears glistening in her mother's eyes made her heart sink. She'd been honest, but at what cost? Hurting a woman she loved beyond measure created an ache in her soul.

"Take it from me, Holly. Holding on to anger is debilitating. It wears you down. I lived it for a very long time. It changes who you are as a person. I don't ever want you to be in such limbo. No matter how long it takes, I'll be here waiting for you."

Holly felt her mother's fingers lightly run through the ends of her hair as she walked away from her and into the stables.

Dylan made his way over to her in a few easy strides. "Is everything okay?" he asked, his brows knitted together.

"It's fine," she answered. Her voice sounded a tad wobbly to her own ears. She was doing all she could not to scream with frustration.

He cocked his head to one side. "You sure about that? Things sounded pretty intense."

Raw emotion clogged her throat. "We're just going through something at the moment."

Keeping her family issues private was a habit she'd perfected during the years when her parents had been mad at the entire town. Furious that town officials hadn't filed charges against Cassidy for the accident, they'd closed ranks and withdrawn from the West Falls community, including Pastor Blake and Main Street Church. As a result, she was accustomed to holding everything in and not confiding in anyone about her family. She'd learned at an early age to close ranks. Old habits die hard, she realized.

Dylan narrowed his eyes as he gazed at her. "I don't know what the problem is, and it's certainly none of my business, but I can tell she loves you very much. They both do. Take it from me. You're real fortunate to have them in your life."

"I know, Dylan," she said with sigh. "But that doesn't mean we don't have our problems."

Dylan shot her a look resembling disbelief. From the outside looking in, her family appeared to be picture-perfect. Dylan had no idea that her family had been embroiled in such a firestorm. Thankfully, things had changed for the better when fences were mended in the aftermath of the big storm. It had taken years for the emotional scars left over from the accident to fade away. And still, the residual affects lingered.

How could she put it all into words and make Dylan understand? She threw her hands up in the air.

"Okay. If you don't believe me, here it is. For eight years my mother kept Cassidy's letters from me and made me think she'd totally turned her back on me when she moved to Phoenix after the accident. Instead, she was reaching out to me and writing heartfelt letters I never got to read."

She fisted her hands in her lap. "Those letters would have meant the world to me at a time when I hit rock bottom. I thought my best friend had abandoned me!"

Dylan let out a low whistle. "That's pretty rough. I can see how that would make your head spin."

She released a deep breath. "Our relationship has always been based on trust. I can't believe my mom would withhold something so important from me."

"Did she tell you why she did it?" Dylan prodded. "She must have thought she had good reason."

"After the accident, she was overwhelmed by pain and fear. Her feelings toward Cassidy were ones of anger and rage. But that's no excuse!" She shuddered as the dark memories swept over her. "It was a horrible time, that's for sure. But it's just so hard for me to accept the lengths she went to out of some misguided desire to protect me."

A tremor rippled along his jawline. He opened his mouth, then shut it. His eyes were focused on her like lasers. Although looking into Dylan's eyes wasn't a hardship, there was something unnerving about his perusal. He was staring at her so intently. She couldn't shake the feeling that he was itching to weigh in on the situation.

She frowned. "What? Why are you looking at me like that?"

He stalled for a moment, chewing on his lip. He narrowed his eyes as he looked at her. "Holly, forgiveness doesn't just work one way," he finally said, his voice low and measured. "If I hadn't forgiven you when I first arrived in West Falls, we probably wouldn't be sitting here right now. And when you made your pact with the roses, you chose to keep information about the accident just among the four of you. Sometimes we all fall short of who we want to be. Perhaps you should remember that when you're dealing with your mother."

Chapter Nine

Holly's reaction to his pointed comment about forgiveness was weighing heavily on Dylan's mind. She hadn't said much in response, making him feel as if he'd overstepped a boundary. Her reddened cheeks and the firm set of her mouth had done all the talking for her. As soon as Frank and Maggie emerged from the stables, she'd quickly excused herself to take care of Picasso. Although his gut instinct was to follow her and make amends, he'd decided to give her some space.

His intention hadn't been to rile her up or get her all twisted up inside. Speaking from the heart, especially to Holly, was second nature to him. More than anything he'd wanted her to realize that her mother's actions were rooted in fear, as much as her own had been when she'd failed to tell him about her being in a wheelchair and in the aftermath of her accident. Fear was not an excuse, but it did sometimes explain lapses in judgment.

Why are you getting so invested in this anyway? Why does it bother you so much that Holly and Maggie are at odds?

In the long run it wasn't something life altering for him. He wouldn't be around long enough to see the fallout. But why did it feel so very important to him? Why was his first instinct to step in and make things better? To help them both heal from their estrangement? Why was he allowing himself to get sucked into their lives?

An hour after his conversation with Holly, Dylan found himself enjoying some downtime in his cottage. After making some popcorn in the microwave, spending some quality time with Leo and taking a long, hot shower, he'd gotten his second wind. Even though it was just a temporary place to rest his head until he left town, he was enjoying the peaceful vibe of his abode. Located near the center of town, it was a cheerful little place with large windows that allowed sunlight to stream effortlessly into the kitchen and living room. He'd made a few fixes to the place—nothing major, just a little paint and spackle. But somehow it was beginning to feel like home. And for a man like him, it felt like a big deal.

Earlier that afternoon, Frank and Maggie had invited him to an event at the ranch this evening, a coming-out of sorts for the horses. He was honored to be included in the festivities. According to the Lynches, it was customary at Horseshoe Bend Ranch to usher in the new horses by putting them on display and inviting friends to stop by and admire them.

"It also gives us a chance to visit with everyone after being on the road for so long," Frank had said with a wink in his wife's direction.

By the time Dylan made his way back to Horseshoe Bend Ranch, a dozen or so people were gathered around the stables. He almost did a double take when he got out of his truck and laid eyes on the nicely decorated table set up in the grassy area next to the stables. A red-and-white checkered tablecloth, small vases filled with lavender and softly flickering lanterns created a festive vibe. The tangy smell of barbecue drifted in his direction, causing a low grumble in his stomach. The aroma made him realize how hungry he was for some down-home cooking.

Several of the ranch hands welcomed him with rau-cous greetings. They were a great group to work with—easygoing, hardworking and friendly. They'd gone out of their way to make him feel as if he was one of them, as if he was a part of Horseshoe Bend Ranch. Strangely enough, he did feel a sense of belonging, and it left a warm, settled feeling in his bones.

He cast his gaze over the area, hoping for a glimpse of Holly. Within seconds his eyes focused in on her. She was sitting a few feet away by the stable doors, her face lit up with joy as she chatted with a tall dark-haired man. Dylan gave him the once-over, honing in on the shiny gold badge attached to his khaki-colored jacket. Something about the way they were talking caused a kernel of discomfort to pass over him. Holly seemed so at ease, so lighthearted. Was there something about this particular man triggering these feelings in her? He shook off his irritation, not enjoying the stab of jealousy slicing through him, leaving his stomach in ribbons.

He felt a little hitch in his heart at the sight of Holly. Instead of her normal T-shirt and jeans, she was wear-ing a burgundy-colored long-sleeved shirt, a denim skirt and a pair of black cowboy boots. Her hair hung in loose waves around her face. A pair of dazzling earrings glittered by her ears. Her gaze locked with his. She sent him a hesitant smile.

In three easy strides he was at her side, drawn in by the welcoming look stamped on her face. He hadn't planned on intruding on her conversation with the lawman, but there was something pulling him in Holly's direction. It was a strong force he couldn't ignore, like a magnet tugging him toward her. There was no point in fighting it, he reckoned.

"Glad you could make it," Holly said as soon as he reached her side.

"Mighty glad to be here this evening," he said, tipping his hat in her direction. "I'm grateful for the invite."

"Cullen Brand." A hand shot out in his direction, and he reached out to shake it, nodding at Cullen as he introduced himself. He had the distinct impression the other man was sizing him up just as much as he was taking stock of the lawman.

"Cullen works with Tate at the sheriff's office. He's a deputy," Holly explained.

"I hear you're just back from Afghanistan, Dylan." Cullen's eyes were alight with interest.

"That's right. I've been back stateside for over a month now. I'm still getting my bearings, though."

"Well, welcome to town. West Falls has a lot to offer."

His gaze shifted back toward Holly, giving Dylan the distinct impression he was making reference to her. "Especially here at Horseshoe Bend Ranch." He looked Dylan straight in the eye, his expression hardening.

"We're a real tight community, too. Always looking out for one another."

"As it should be," Dylan drawled, meeting Cullen's unwavering stare head-on.

"Cullen!" Tate's voice carried across the yard. He was motioning for him to come over. Cullen acknowledged him with a wave before excusing himself to go join him. Dylan shook his head in disbelief as Cullen walked away from them. When he turned back toward Holly, he noticed the corners of her mouth were twitching with laughter. "Don't mind Cullen. He's a little protective of me." She covered her mouth with her hand in an attempt to hide her amusement.

"Did the two of you date or something?" he asked gruffly. Again, his gut tightened at the thought of Cullen and Holly's seemingly close relationship. It was a distinctly uncomfortable feeling.

"No, we never dated. He's just a good friend. And an all-around great guy."

The pressure in his chest loosened up so that it no longer felt uncomfortable. The thought of Cullen and Holly being more than friends didn't sit well with him. With Holly's reassuring words, he began to relax again.

"I hope what I said earlier about your mother didn't upset you." He studied her face, looking for any signs of distress.

Holly shook her head. "I wasn't upset. Not with you anyway." She twisted her lips. "I was pretty mad at myself, though. And embarrassed. You held a mirror up to me, and I was forced to take a long look at myself. For months now I've been angry at Mama for keeping information from me, but I did the very same thing to you. Not to mention that the roses and I kept a huge secret for eight years about the cause of the accident. How could I not have seen that I was holding her to a different standard than myself?"

"Sometimes we're too close to a situation to see it clearly. Don't beat yourself up about it. It happens to the best of us."

She looked away from him. "You must think I'm a hypocrite. 'Judge not, that you be not judged.' I've read that scripture dozens of times, yet I've failed to practice it in my own life."

His heart cracked a little at her somber tone, coupled with the lost expression on her face. A strong urge to console her swept over him.

"Listen, Holly, I'm the last one to point any fingers at anyone. My relationship with my father is a train wreck. For most of my life I've been angry at him because all I ever wanted was for him to be present in my life. And he wasn't." He paused for a moment, determined to stave off a rising tide of emotions. "You've got something special. Two parents who are involved in your day-to-day world and who love you. All I was trying to say is, don't let anything get in the way of that. It's a beautiful thing."

Her shoulders sagged. She looked frustrated and defeated.

"I know what you're saying is true, but I'm just not there yet. In my own way and in my own time, I'll patch things up with Mama."

Dylan reached out and captured her chin in his palm. He stroked her jaw with his fingers, enjoying the feel of her silky-smooth skin. "Just don't wait too long, okay?

My mama used to tell me not to let the sun go down on my anger."

Holly cocked her head to the side, her brow furrowed. "Did you always listen to her?"

"Nope," he said with a chuckle. "I was an ornery little fella. A few times she had to wash my mouth out with soap due to my sassing her."

"Thanks. Now I've got that image in my head," Holly said with a smirk. She began laughing, which caused Dylan to chortle even louder at the memory of his pint-size self. She threw her head back and clutched her belly, her face contorted with merriment.

A feeling of joy slid through him until he was filled to overflowing with it. It was moments like this, when it was just the two of them, that it seemed as if all was right with the world. And it felt as if this was all he would ever need to be perfectly, deliriously happy.

By the time the sun began to slide beneath the horizon, two dozen or so people were gathered at the ranch. Tate, Cassidy, Doc Sampson, Jenna, Pastor Blake and his wife were some of the faces he recognized, as well as Frank and Maggie. Holly introduced him to the local vet, Vicky Shepard, and her husband, Tom. Everyone gathered around the table and feasted on barbecued ribs and chicken, corn on the cob, baked beans, biscuits and peach cobbler. Even though he didn't know everyone, he felt at ease in their company, as if they were old friends with whom he was getting reacquainted.

After dinner Maggie invited everyone to head toward the arena. It was lit up with lanterns and twinkling lights. There were six horses in all being led inside. Three Arabians, one chestnut, two onyx. The other three were bay-colored American quarter horses. It was a sight more breathtaking than any he'd ever seen. Each was more beautiful and graceful than the next.

Holly was radiant. As much as he found himself captivated by the horses, he found his gaze straying toward her. His sweet, beautiful Holly.

"This is incredible," he said. "I've never seen so many fine horses all at once!"

"Believe it or not, it moves me every single time," Holly gushed. "I can't even count how many runnings of the horses I've witnessed, but each and every one is special."

Frank walked by, leading an Arabian. He stopped right next to them, a glint in his eyes as he addressed Dylan. "We have a tradition around here. Since you're our newest hire, we'd like you to showcase one of the horses. His name's Warrior. I think it's pretty fitting."

Frank held out the reins to him. His smile was full of encouragement. For a moment Dylan was frozen, unable to reach out and take Frank's offering. He swiveled his head toward Holly, filled with disbelief at the gesture.

"Go on, Dylan," Holly urged. "What are you waiting for?"

She gave him a nudge. Dylan took the leather straps, running his fingers over them for a moment before guiding Warrior into the arena and mounting him. Once he sat astride the Arabian, Dylan cast a quick glance in Holly's direction, his pulse quickening as their gazes locked. She was clapping for him and the other riders, her face lit up with happiness. His heart seized up at the sight of her.

Against every instinct warning him not to get too

invested in his temporary life in West Falls, he was becoming tethered to Horseshoe Bend Ranch and all its inhabitants. As each day rolled into the next, it was becoming harder and harder to imagine himself leaving this wonderful place. And most of all, saying goodbye to Holly.

Watching Dylan mount Warrior and then lead him in a trot around the arena caused a fierce swell of emotion to course through her. Together they were pure poetry in motion. Her cowboy soldier. He was constantly surprising her, just when she thought she knew him like the back of her hand. The restrained emotion he'd shown just before taking Warrior's reins had almost done her in. His expression had been full of gratitude. Why had he been so surprised by her father's gesture? Why had he acted as if he didn't deserve it?

More than anything in the world, she'd wanted to share this special moment with Dylan, to see it reflected through his eyes. And she'd seen it all—the wonder, the admiration, his deep love of horses—shining back at her. He'd gotten choked up when her father asked him to ride one of the Arabians because of the respect he had for Horseshoe Bend Ranch.

Dylan got it. He understood her family's passion. He had reverence for the horses and livestock. Some people were simply impressed with Horseshoe Bend Ranch and the grandeur and majesty of it. Dylan saw past the surface. He was all about the horses and the day-to-day running of the ranch. The lifestyle. Those values went way down deep to his very core.

The sound of boots rustling in the dirt had her swiveling around. Malachi was standing there, his gaze transfixed by the horses trotting around the arena. She grabbed him by the arm. "Malachi! You're back. How's your grandfather?"

He winced, letting out a slow hiss of air before he responded. "He passed on to a better world. We had his burial earlier today."

Holly knew enough about Native American traditions to know the ceremony had been sacred and simple. She reached out and placed her hand in his, squeezing it gently.

"Oh, Malachi. I'm so sorry. I know how much he meant to you. He practically raised you."

A slight tremor danced along his jawline. "I was glad to be there with him in the end as he drew his last breath. He lived a good life. That's all that really matters in the end. And the things we take away from our loved ones. The lessons they leave behind."

"I'm sure Jacob left you with enough of his wisdom to sustain you for the rest of your life."

"What he taught me most is that life is too short to be afraid." He turned toward her, staring at her pointedly. "I think that's something we have in common, Holly. Fear."

"You? Afraid?" Holly scoffed. "I can't ever remember you being intimidated by a single thing."

Malachi grimaced. "It seems that way, doesn't it? Sure, I can tackle a rattlesnake head-on and break in a wild horse, but when it comes to opening myself up… to a woman…that's where I let the fear take over."

"What do you have to be afraid of?" she asked, swallowing past the huge lump in her throat. It suddenly dawned on her that Malachi avoided relationships like the plague. Why hadn't she ever asked him about it? For the life of her, she couldn't remember the last time he'd had a woman in his life.

"Rejection. Opening myself up to someone who can hurt me again."

Again? When had Malachi's heart been broken? And by whom? She crossed her hands in front of her, fiddling with her thumbs as her mind raced. "And you think I'm like you?"

Malachi leaned down and brushed a kiss across her cheek. "I think you might believe you're not good enough, just like me. But from where I'm standing, there's nobody better than you."

Tears filled Holly's eyes as the beautiful compliment washed over her. Malachi smiled at her and ambled away, heading straight toward Tate and Cassidy. She watched through misty eyes as Malachi delivered his news, and Cassidy and Tate hugged him. She loved this man like a brother, yet until this very moment, she'd been clueless about his doubts and fears. And his heartache. It was so true that you never knew the burdens people carried around with them.

"One ice-cold lemonade for the pretty lady." Suddenly Dylan was standing in front of her, offering her a glass. While she was busy talking to Malachi, he must have finished up in the arena. She'd been so consumed by their conversation that she hadn't even noticed.

Dylan took one look at her and frowned. "Hey, what's wrong? Why are you crying?"

"Malachi's back. He was just telling me his grandfather passed away." She wiped a tear away from her cheek.

Dylan got down on his haunches, setting the drink on the ground beside him. "I'm awful sorry to hear that. Losing someone is never easy."

"I'll be praying for Malachi and his family. Now, more than ever, it makes me realize I really need to set things straight with Mama. I don't want to live in regret. If something ever happened to her, and I hadn't fixed things—"

He clutched her hand. "Nothing's going to happen to her. Talk to her tonight and tell her how you feel. Don't let another day go by without forgiving her, especially if it's weighing this heavily on your mind."

She nodded. "I will. For sure. As soon as the evening winds down, I'll talk to her."

He reached up and grazed her cheek with his palm. "Hey, what can I do to bring back that gorgeous smile of yours? I don't like seeing you so sad."

"I'll be fine. I just got a reality check, that's all," she reassured him, reaching out and brushing her knuckles against his hand. The desire to touch him, to connect with him, was overwhelming. Yet it took all of her courage to initiate contact with him. Malachi was right. The fear of rejection still lived close to the surface. Thanks to Dylan and his rock-solid presence, those fears were slowly fading.

"Hey, c'mere, Holly. I want to show you something."

Dylan gestured for her to follow him as he walked past the stables and headed toward the pasture. The area was peaceful, with not a single person in sight. He walked right up to the fence and threw his head back, causing his cowboy hat to come tumbling down to the ground. He stretched out his arms and looked up toward the heavens. Glancing back over his shoulder, he grinned at her, then pointed up at the full moon dazzling an otherwise onyx sky.

Watching Dylan revel in the beautiful fall evening was a humbling experience. She'd lived on this ranch her entire life, and although she loved it, she knew there were times she took it for granted. He'd told her enough about his time in Afghanistan for her to truly appreciate what the great outdoors meant to him. Clean air. Wide-open spaces. Freedom. Safety.

She was in awe of the way he appreciated the simple things that couldn't be bought or sold. Of the way he could rejoice in God's most wondrous creations and show such sincere gratitude for all his blessings. As she gazed at him, her mind and her heart felt full, almost to the point of overflowing. And she knew in this moment no other man would ever do, because Dylan was wedged firmly in her soul. For now and always.

Holly followed behind him, maneuvering herself over to the fence until she was parked beside where he stood. She was smiling now, which was a good thing. It had been painful to see her with tears in her eyes. It made him realize he'd do anything to make her feel better. And who wouldn't feel their spirits lift by looking up at this incredible full moon? Who wouldn't feel buoyed by this beautiful backdrop? It was a reminder of how insignificant they all were in the scheme of things. Their problems were nothing compared to the celestial splendor of the sky.

He couldn't remember a time in his life when he'd felt so content. For so long he'd had this feeling of unhappiness lodged inside his chest. He hadn't even realized until recently how much it was weighing him down. Ever since he'd arrived in West Falls, those feelings had begun to dissipate, like fog lifting after the rain. He felt almost weightless. Content.

"The look on your face when you're here in your element… It's pure joy," Holly said. "I've spent my life around cowboys. Not all of them light up from the inside when they're working the ranch. Not all of them feel what you feel when they're surrounded by nothing more than land and sky and horses."

"I come from a long line of ranchers on my dad's side. I think it runs through my veins," he said, acknowledging for the first time his ranching ties.

"Whether you realize it or not, Dylan, you've found your sweet spot." She grinned at him, appearing delighted at the prospect of him finding his way.

He was just happy he'd gotten her to smile. "I think you're right," he acknowledged. "For so long I resisted it, this gravitational pull toward ranching. That was one of the reasons I enlisted. I was so afraid of being like my dad, so scared I'd turn out to be his carbon copy. I wanted to go down a road he'd never traveled."

He shuddered, suddenly overcome by a feeling of vulnerability. "But here I am again. Right back where I started."

"Just because you love ranching doesn't mean you're like him. It just means you're a cowboy, down to the bone. He doesn't own that."

"I know that here." He tapped the side of his temple.

"But here." He placed his palm over his heart. "That's where the doubts live. And sometimes they rattle around my brain until I can't even think straight."

Holly nodded her head, her expression full of understanding. "I get it. That happens to me sometimes, too. The voice of doubt in your head becomes louder than your own instincts. When those thoughts creep in, I just have to focus on something to center me."

She reached out and placed her hand on the fence enclosure. "Most times it's Horseshoe Bench Ranch that settles me. Being here reminds me of what's truly important."

There was a wistful feeling rising up inside him as he listened to Holly's words. His gaze focused on a place far in the distance. "Lately I've been thinking more and more about my dreams of owning my own ranch."

He cast a quick glance in her direction, needing to see her reaction to his statement. More times than he could count, his dreams had been scoffed at and deemed out of his reach, so much so that he no longer shared them. Confiding his aspirations to Holly wasn't easy. It left him wide-open.

"Nothing as grand as your family's spread," he qualified, "but something all of my own. A legacy for my children. Something they can feel proud to be a part of."

Children. He'd gone and said it out loud. That desire was something he'd wrestled with for some time. As much as he wanted to experience being a parent, there was still so much doubt about whether or not he would be a good one. For him, fatherhood seemed like this elusive thing he couldn't quite put his finger on. It was a mystery he wasn't sure he could unravel.

"Oh, Dylan, that's wonderful," Holly said, enthusiasm laced in her voice. "I may be biased, but owning a ranch, working the land and seeing it grow into something more beautiful than you ever imagined… That's as good as it gets."

It was as if she was reading his thoughts. Truthfully, he couldn't imagine a better life. Unless, of course, that life included a woman with whom he could share those aspirations. Someone he could cleave to for the rest of his days, the way the good Lord intended. That would be a fulfilling life.

Holly bit her lip, her expression thoughtful. "Having children is something I think about all the time. I'm not sure if I'll ever be able to have a child of my own, but if I could, it would be a dream come true."

Although he'd wondered if Holly was able to bear children, he never would have asked such a delicate question. But now that she'd brought it up herself, he could tell her how he felt about the subject. "I can't imagine you not being a mother someday. Your outlook on life is incredible. You'd bring so much to a child's life. Hope. Kindness. Faith. And most of all, an abundance of love. You deserve to live out that dream."

"Thank you," Holly whispered, emotion shimmering in her eyes. "Coming from you, that means a lot."

Dylan reached out and clasped Holly's hand in his, enjoying the way their hands felt wrapped together.

He looked up at the endless stretch of sky. Set against a velvet backdrop, the luminescent moon sat surrounded by twinkling, dancing stars. He sucked in a deep breath, inhaling the clean country air.

"It doesn't make any sense at all, but somehow the

moon seems bigger here, and I don't ever think I've seen a sky so picture-perfect. Being here at the ranch settles me. It makes me feel as if anything is possible. I feel centered," he said.

He turned toward her, admiring the way the moon gleamed off her dewy skin. "That's in large part due to you."

Her eyes widened and her mouth curved in a sweet smile.

"Me? I haven't done anything."

"Haven't you?" he asked, his voice a low whisper. "I beg to differ. You've changed my whole world."

Holly's expression was one of pure joy. He leaned over and brushed the side of her face with his knuckles. Their eyes met, and for an instant, he saw something so beautiful and pure in their depths. It took his breath away. He dipped his head down and captured her lips in a tender, romantic kiss.

As his lips moved over hers, he felt a powerful stirring inside his chest. He wanted this kiss to go on and on until the sun crept up over the horizon. She was kissing him back with a gentleness he'd never experienced before in his life. She was cracking his heart wide-open in the process.

As the kiss ended, he found it hard to pull away from her. For long seconds he just laid his forehead against hers. From the moment he'd found out Holly was in a wheelchair, he'd resisted the magnetic pull in her direction, even though he'd felt it from the moment he'd read her first letter. Since he'd arrived in West Falls, he'd been fighting their attraction with everything he had in him. But it seemed as if every time he dug in his heels, something happened to show him how wrong he was to deny the way she made him feel.

Was it wise of him to get so close to her when he knew his time in West Falls was limited? He wasn't sure. Sometimes feelings trumped wisdom, he realized, particularly when you were with someone who made you feel things you hadn't felt in a very long time. If ever.

Holly was biting down on her lip, cheeks flushed, her eyes shining brightly. "Was that a friends-only kiss?"

"Friends don't usually kiss by the light of the moon," he teased.

He was feeling cocky, buoyed by their amazing kiss. It gave him a rush sharing something so sweet and wonderful with Holly. He'd dreamed of moments like this while he was in Afghanistan, in the quiet hours between darkness and dawn. The reality was far better than his dreams.

"I always want us to be friends, Dylan. No matter what." Her voice rang out with a sincerity he couldn't ignore. She held out her hand. "Shake on it?"

Suppressing the urge to grin, he got down on his haunches and clasped it in a firm handshake. "I promise we'll always be friends."

Holly let out a relieved sigh, her mouth creasing into the beginnings of a smile.

"But something tells me we're headed toward something way more special," he said.

As the fireflies danced in the cool night air, Dylan took off his denim jacket and draped it around Holly's shoulders. He leaned in so their shoulders were touching, then placed his arm around her. He wanted to be close to her, because being with her was the one thing that made everything else fade away. It was the thing that made the most sense. All the doubts and second-guessing seemed to vanish in a puff of smoke whenever he just focused on her and stopped worrying about the future.

With a lifetime of imperfect moments in his past, this night with Holly was shaping up to be a memorable one. As impossible as he knew it was, he wished he could capture the moment in a bottle for all time. That way he could go back and uncork the bottle whenever he had the urge, allowing the memories of this evening to wash over him like a warm summer shower.

As euphoric as he felt, as deeply satisfied as he'd ever been in his life, he had a niggling feeling in the pit of his stomach. Try as he might, he couldn't seem to make it go away. Something told him that this rare feeling of contentment wasn't going to last.

As the celebration drew to a close, Dylan asked her if he could drive her back to the main house. Without skipping a beat, she accepted his offer. Being courted by her cowboy soldier was a heady experience. He'd barely left her side all night. She got goose pimples when his arm brushed against hers as they sat side by side in his truck. Joy speared through her as they sang along in unison to the chart-topping hit on the radio.

When they reached the house, they sat on the porch for a spell, listening to the quiet sounds of a Texas evening. The howl of a coyote rang out in the stillness, cutting through the silence. Dylan reached out and laced his fingers through her own. It had been ages since she'd held hands this way with someone who made her heart skip a beat. It had been so long since she'd felt this in tune with another human being. Many days she'd doubted whether it would ever happen for her.

When Dylan finally saw her to the door, he bent down and brushed a kiss across her cheek, then rubbed his thumb alongside her jawline. "I'd like to take you to the rodeo on Friday night. As my date."

All night she'd been hoping he would ask her. At one point she'd almost swallowed her pride and asked him to go with her. The annual rodeo, held out at the fairgrounds, was a two-day event that drew in crowds from all across the state. The only rodeo she'd ever missed was the one held a few months after her accident.

Being asked on a date by Dylan was a dream come true. Most twenty-six-year-old women took things like this for granted. But not her. The last time she'd been asked out on a date had been in high school. Her outings with Cullen didn't really count, since they'd never made it past friendship. As attractive as he was and as much as she enjoyed his company, she'd never felt for him one iota of what Dylan sparked inside her. There had been no pull in his direction, no tugging at her heartstrings.

"That would be great, Dylan." She could feel a huge sappy grin overtaking her face, but at the moment, she didn't even care. How could she not smile at the prospect of spending an evening in Dylan's company? Better yet, as his date.

Dylan smiled back at her, a self-assured grin that made her think he'd been counting on a yes.

"See you tomorrow?" He said it like a question. She simply smiled and nodded her head, secure in the knowledge that they would make time to see each other at some point during the day.

Finally they said their goodbyes, even though she felt a strong impulse to stretch the evening out until the stars were stamped out from the velvet sky. Dylan seemed reluctant, also. He kept turning around to look back at her as he made his way off the front porch and into his truck. Once she was inside the house, she listened for the sound of its engine roaring to life as he vanished into the night.

She couldn't remember a time when she'd felt so hopeful. So wonderfully alive. This evening had been full of fellowship and romance. Lots and lots of romance. And there had been such tenderness in the moments she'd shared with Dylan. His denim coat was still wrapped around her shoulders, serving as a reminder of his chivalry. The best thing about being with Dylan was that he never made her feel helpless. Most important of all, he acknowledged all the things she was capable of doing. He didn't treat her as if she were broken.

A pang coursed through her as she remembered one of the things they'd discussed. *Children.* Listening to him talk about his future was an eye-opener. Carrying a child to full term was difficult for paraplegics. In order to conceive, she might have to go off most of her medications. She'd done the research and talked to her doctor at length about the possibility of someday having a child. Although she had a referral to a top specialist in the field, she'd been putting it off, nervous about the prospect of flying to Boston by herself for the consultation.

A huge sigh bubbled up inside her. Ever since the accident she'd refused to fly alone. The very thought of it triggered an anxious response, a panicky feeling that raced straight through her, leaving her breathless and perspiring. On the few occasions she'd flown, her father had accompanied her. Although she'd been grateful at the time, she couldn't help but wonder if his protectiveness had held her back. How could she even think about raising a child if she couldn't stand on her own two feet and face her fears?

And how could she even hope for a future with Dylan when she wasn't certain she could ever give him the children he dreamed of making part of his legacy?

Chapter Ten

The following day passed by in a flurry of activity at Horseshoe Bend Ranch. There was an undercurrent of excitement as the buzz surrounding the rodeo reached a fever pitch. Holly didn't come across anyone—not a ranch hand nor a wrangler—who wasn't itching to attend. She didn't know a soul in town who wouldn't be putting in an appearance at the two-day event, including her three best friends. Although she'd promised to meet up with the roses, something told her there was bound to be a big reaction from them when they saw her with Dylan. They were going to tease her for sure, especially since she'd told them they were simply friends. Just the thought of it brought a smile to her face.

After her riding lesson with Malachi, she was able to spend some time with Dylan as he groomed Picasso in the stables. It was nice to be around someone without having to work in order to fill up the silence. Everything flowed so easily between them, even the quiet moments. Before Dylan headed off to the northern pasture to repair fences, they finalized their plans for the evening. He told her he'd pick her up at the main house a little before six o'clock.

The remainder of the day passed quickly, leaving her with little or no time to fret about her outfit or to get nervous about her first date in eight years.

But before she could allow herself to fully enjoy the evening ahead, she needed to make amends with her mother. She'd tossed and turned all night just thinking about their estrangement and her own unwillingness to grant forgiveness. She didn't want to be the type of person who harbored grudges, particularly against someone she loved with all her heart.

At this time of day, she knew where her mother could easily be found. As Holly maneuvered her chair across the side lawn, she spotted her mother in the distance, up to her elbows in mulch and compost in her garden. When she came closer, her mother whirled around, a surprised expression etched on her face. "Holly! I'm surprised to see you out here."

Holly's heart sank. There was a time when her mother wouldn't have been startled at all to see her in the garden. It showed just how wide the gap was between them. Gone were the days when she'd just show up unexpectedly with a glass of sweet tea and lemon bars.

"I've always loved this place and being able to see your green thumb in action. What are you planting?"

Her mother wiped her brow with her gloved hand. "Just trying to plant these wildflower seeds next. Blue bonnets will add a nice touch to the garden. They need a sunny spot in order to thrive. I finished with the pansies and violas. And of course my favorites, snapdragons." She looked up at Holly, squinting against the sun's glare.

"Is something troubling you, sweetheart?"

Holly swallowed past the lump in her throat. There was so much she wanted to say, yet she didn't know where to start. She folded her hands in her lap and fumbled with her fingers.

"I'm tired of being angry at you. I've been blaming you for all the lost years with Cassidy. But the truth is, you weren't solely responsible for that. There were so many ripples after the accident. It was like a domino effect that toppled down everything in its path."

Tears freely ran down Holly's face, and she didn't even bother to wipe them away.

Her mother's face crumpled. "I did an awful thing. I should never have kept those letters from you. You had every right to read them and decide for yourself if you wanted Cassidy in your life."

Holly nodded. "Yes, it was wrong, Mama. But I forgive you. And I know why you did it. You were protecting me the only way you knew how. Someday I hope to be a mother myself. From what I've heard, protecting one's child is a strong instinct."

"Yes, it is," she acknowledged with a nod. "It's the most powerful force on earth. But in the past few years I've come to realize you don't need me or Tate or anyone else to fight your battles. You've grown into a strong, independent and wise young woman, Holly Lynch. And I'm so very proud to call you my daughter."

Her mother swiftly bridged the gap between them. Holly threw herself into her mother's open arms like a force of nature. It felt so nice to be embracing her mother without a single issue standing between them.

Now there was nothing but love and mutual admiration pulsing in the air around them.

As they broke away from one another, Holly watched as her mother swiped at her eyes with the back of her hand. They were happy tears, born of reconciliation and hope. It was a joyful moment, especially in the aftermath of so much heartache and loss.

"So I heard Dylan talking about taking you to the rodeo tonight." A sweet smile hovered on her mother's lips. She nodded her head approvingly.

Holly couldn't hold back her grin. Suddenly it felt as if all was right in her world. Now that she'd bridged the gap with her mother, her thoughts were full to overflowing about her date with Dylan.

"Our first real date," she said. "I have to admit I'm a little nervous, but more than anything, I'm excited to take this journey with him, wherever it leads."

Her mother reached out and tightly clasped Holly's hand. "It's what your father and I want for you, Holly. To continue to make strides and move forward on your journey. If you decide to follow that path with Dylan at your side, we'll support you."

Holly felt her cheeks flush with excitement. There were no guarantees about her future with Dylan, but she had every reason to believe they were headed toward something wonderful. Knowing she had her parents' blessing made it even more special. Anticipation about this evening was building inside of her, as fragile and precious as a burgeoning flower in springtime.

When Dylan arrived at the house at five minutes before six, Holly was there to greet him. He was standing on her front porch with a bouquet of wildflowers in his hands, dressed in a dark pair of jeans, a long-sleeved shirt and a black cowboy hat.

"I've been wanting to give you flowers for a long time," he drawled. His grin made him even more handsome than anyone had a right to be. She had to tear her gaze away from him or run the risk of staring as if she were a kid looking through the candy store window.

She reached for the flowers, raising them so she could inhale their sweet scent.

"Thank you. This is way better than the first time," she said, making reference to the flowers he'd inadvertently given to Cassidy on the day they'd met.

Dylan laughed and shook his head. She felt happy he could look back on that moment and chuckle about it. At the time it hadn't been a laughing matter. Things had changed so much between them in the past few weeks. It was humbling to acknowledge she'd made such a major mistake with Dylan, yet he was still in her life.

As her parents looked on with barely contained excitement, she sailed out the door with Dylan, eager to get to the rodeo and start enjoying the festivities. It was more practical for her to drive since her van was tailored to her specifications and she had a placard designating her as a disabled driver. With the placard, they'd be able to park close to the venue so she wouldn't have to travel all the way across the dusty, uneven lot. Being in a wheelchair meant having to plan every aspect of an outing, from the parking situation to making sure the seats were wheelchair accessible.

From the moment they entered the gates, they could see the atmosphere at the rodeo was lively and bustling with spectators. It was a little tricky at times navigating her way through the sea of people, but Dylan was a huge asset. With his commanding height, broad shoulders and no-nonsense demeanor, he easily cut a path for them through the crowd, never leaving her side for a moment.

By the time they made it to their seats, the first event—barrel racing—was about to start. Holly was rooting for West Fall's own, Lacy Kidd, one of the strongest competitors. She cheered loudly along with Dylan as Lacy outperformed all the other riders and was awarded first prize. Bronc riding, bull riding and steer wrestling quickly followed, making for a thrilling event. When Dylan put his arm around her and asked her if she wanted to go get some refreshments, she almost had to pinch herself. Spending time with him at the rodeo was the most fun she'd had in a very long while. Their rapport was effortless, and she couldn't help but feel as if she'd known him her whole life. There was no nervousness, no awkwardness during her first date in eight years. Being with him made her feel as comfortable in her own skin as she'd ever been since the accident.

When her stomach started grumbling loudly as they made their way toward the concession stand, they both broke out in laughter. It was funny how she didn't even feel embarrassed. She felt so comfortable with him, so natural. It was the way her brother had always described the ease he felt whenever he was with Cassidy.

Dylan suddenly stopped in his tracks. When she looked up at him, his entire face had been transformed. His jaw was tight. Stress lines had formed around his eyes. Her eyes quickly skimmed over him. A few moments ago he'd been having a wonderful time. What had caused such a drastic change in him?

"What is it? Is something wrong?"

"It's nothing. I just want to get out of here," he said. His tone was abrupt. His face had an ashen look. It seemed as if he might snap in two.

"Something happened. Tell me. It's written all over your face." She wasn't letting this go, not when she sensed something was terribly wrong.

"Dylan." At the sound of the deep masculine voice, Holly swiveled her head just in time to see a man reach out and grab Dylan by the arm. She watched as Dylan violently jerked away from the man's grip, his face contorted in anger. The older man was tall, broad shouldered, with a full head of sandy-brown hair. Tension crackled in the air as they faced each other, both holding fierce expressions.

Holly reached out and gripped Dylan by the wrist, pulling him toward her in the process. When he turned toward her, his eyebrows were furrowed, his cheeks reddened.

"What's going on? Who is this?" She darted a look at the man, who was still standing a few feet away, his expression as tension filled as Dylan's. Matter of fact, he bore a strong resemblance to Dylan—same eye color, a similar build, the exact same dimple in the chin. Suddenly, bells were clanging in her head.

"Nothing. Nobody." Dylan's tone was clipped and riddled with barely suppressed rage. An angry vein thrummed above his eyebrow. He looked as if he was coming undone.

"Dylan. Please. Tell me the truth. What's got you so

twisted up inside?" She was begging him now, filled with fear and uncertainty about his state of mind. Something had to have happened to create such a change in him. What in the world was going on?

Dear Lord, please hear my prayer. Whatever war is raging inside Dylan, please give me the tools and the wisdom to help him through it. I care so deeply for him, and it hurts me to see him so torn up inside. With Your guidance, we can get through this.

His face hardened into a mask of granite. His eyes were bristling with anger, his teeth gritted. He jerked his chin in the man's direction as he spit out, "That's R. J. McDermott, owner of the Bar M Ranch." He shoved his fists into his pockets and looked away from her. "He also happens to be my father."

Tension crackled in the air in the wake of his announcement. He swung his gaze back toward Holly, needing to see her reaction to his admission. The look of shock and pity on Holly's face made him want to turn on his cowboy-booted heel and leave the fairgrounds. Even though he wanted to get as far away from R. J. McDermott as humanly possible, he couldn't very well leave Holly behind. And he was sick and tired of running away from things. So far, it hadn't done him any good.

"Son, please just give me a few minutes." He couldn't remember ever hearing such a pleading tone in his father's voice. He almost sounded human. For a moment he almost thought R.J.'s expression was one of humility. Surely he must be seeing things, since there wasn't anything humble about his father.

He left out a harsh laugh. "Why should I? That's a

lot more than you ever gave me." He pointed his chin in his father's direction. "What do you want?"

"I've been trying to find you for years, ever since you left Madden. I heard you were in the service, but your mama wouldn't give me any information about where you were stationed."

"Don't talk about my mother." His voice rang out sharply. "You don't have the right."

R.J. held up his hands as if warding off an enraged bull. "I know you're angry at me. And you have every right to be. For a very long time I didn't do the right thing. I'm hoping to change all that."

Seeing his father after such a long time was a shock to the system. It rocked him to his core. He hadn't expected it in a million years. Not here of all places. Not in West Falls, miles and miles away from Oklahoma. He'd believed his father had written him off years ago.

What was he doing here? How had he tracked him down?

"Dylan. Son. Hear me out." Hearing the word *son* roll off his father's tongue made him grit his teeth even harder.

Looking at R. J. McDermott was like staring into a mirror. They shared the same sea-green eyes, a similar rugged build, the exact dimple in their chins and identical noses. Because of the striking resemblance, his paternity had become a hotly debated topic in his hometown. Although his mama's advice had been to hold his head up high and ignore the petty gossip and whispers, it hadn't been easy.

Seeing his father again forced him to relive those soul-crushing moments. It reminded him of every slight, every snub, every father-son event he'd missed out on as a kid. It brought back the pain of having to witness his father sitting with his wife and other kids in the front pew at church while he'd hidden himself in the back. And he'd never forget all the fights he'd waged in his mother's honor when some kid had called her a foul name. It had all been because of R. J. McDermott and his shaky moral compass.

A muscle twitched in his jaw. His stood up tall, steeling himself against the onslaught of painful memories. He wanted to appear as impenetrable as granite. "There's nothing you could ever say to me to make up for everything you put me through."

R.J.'s mouth twisted. "But I'd like to try. That's why I hired a private detective to find you. Because I want to be in your life. I want to build a relationship with you."

"Since when?" he demanded.

His father winced. "Son, I've always loved you. I may not have shown it in the ways that mattered, but I've loved you since the day you were born."

He let out a snort. "You've been in and out of my life since the day I was born. We don't even share the same last name. Any number of times you could have claimed me. You didn't!"

Dylan took a few steps until he was nose to nose with his father.

"So what's changed? Why are you so all fired up about us reconciling? Why now?"

His father's chin trembled. "Because I realized how wrong I've been. I've done a lot of soul-searching. I heard through the grapevine you'd enlisted. For years I've been filled with worry about whether you were going to make it back home alive. It killed me knowing that the only information I had about you came from a few of your high school buddies. And even then, the information was sketchy. Life doesn't often give us second chances. I mean to make the most of mine. If you'll let me."

For a moment he stood and stared into his father's eyes, noticing for the first time how the past six years had aged him. There were tiny wrinkles surrounding his mouth, and his sandy hair was peppered with a few strands of gray.

For his entire life R. J. McDermott had seemed larger than life. Now he seemed vulnerable. Even though he'd always seemed like a giant to Dylan, he was merely a man. The very notion had him questioning everything he thought he knew. It made his thoughts and emotions feel jumbled. Wanting to get as far away as possible from the situation, he took a step backward, coming up against Holly's wheelchair in the process. Turning toward her, he could see the confused expression on her face. "Holly, let's go. There's nothing more I need to hear from him."

Holly looked up at him, her blue eyes wide. "Are you sure? He came all this way to see you."

"Son, please don't go," his father pleaded.

"I'm not your son. You made that mighty clear six years ago."

"You'll always be my son."

"Go back to Oklahoma," he answered.

"I'm not going anywhere, Dylan! Not until the two of us can hash things out." The sound of his father's deep voice was thunderous.

Making sure Holly was right beside him, Dylan charged away from his father and headed toward the exits. It wasn't until he was a good distance away that he finally allowed himself to release the choppy breath he'd been holding.

Dylan's powerful tread made it hard for her to keep up with him as he strode toward the parking lot. His steps were full of anger—an unbridled rage that might have frightened her if it wasn't Dylan she was observing. She knew he wouldn't take it out on her. His emotion went inward. He was a quiet storm brewing. It had nothing to do with her and everything to do with his unexpected run-in with his father.

It was all so confusing. Dylan's father was R. J. Mc-Dermott, the same man who'd hired him at the Bar M Ranch and mentored him in the ways of ranching. But he was also the man who'd refused to give his son the family name or any acknowledgment of his paternity. Yet he was here in West Falls after hiring a private detective, begging his estranged son to give him another chance. Even though she resented him for every scar he'd inflicted on Dylan, she couldn't help but nurture a fragile hope about reconciliation between father and son. Judging from the mutinous expression on Dylan's face, the likelihood of it happening was slim to none.

The facts were still whirling all around her. She was trying to make sense of it, to put the pieces of the puzzle together. Dylan and R.J. Father and son. Six long years of estrangement.

"Dylan, are you all right?" They'd reached her van, and instead of moving toward the passenger side, he was just standing there staring off into space. He was breathing heavily through his nose, his jaw tightly clenched. His face looked as ominous as a storm-filled sky.

"I'm fine," he said with a small nod of his head. "I just couldn't stay in there a minute longer, listening to him."

"I have to admit I'm a little confused. You said a while back that you worked at the Bar M. That's where you learned all about ranching and breaking in wild horses, wasn't it?"

Dylan nodded, which gave her the go-ahead to keep talking. "If your relationship with him was so fractured, how did all that happen?"

Shoving his hands in his pockets, he began pacing back and forth, his cowboy boots stirring up a cloud of dust. "When I was a teenager, he gave me a job, taught me about ranching. I guess you could say he took me under his wing. But he never acknowledged me as his son. He never gave me that sense of belonging, even though I wanted it more than anything. Even though the whole town knew and gossiped about the situation, he never publicly claimed me, never once offered me the McDermott family name."

Seeing the pain etched on Dylan's face was agonizing. Hearing the ragged, broken tone of his voice brought tears to her eyes. She couldn't imagine someone not claiming this wonderful, brave man. How could R. J. McDermott have denied his own son his place in the world? She didn't have to ask what it had done to Dylan. The emotions rippling across his face and laced in the ragged tone of his voice spoke volumes.

"Yet, you ask, why should not the son suffer for the

iniquity of the father?" The scripture from Ezekiel roared through her mind. It was so unfair the price Dylan had paid for his father's pride and selfishness. Because of R. J. McDermott's unwillingness to acknowledge his son, Dylan had been forced to pay for his father's sins. And he was still paying, judging from the torment he was going through. He was still suffering. She knew from her own painful experience that some wounds might never fully heal. But she was a firm believer that with faith and love all things were possible.

Her mouth felt as dry as sawdust. "What happened six years ago?"

He shoved his hands in his back pockets and rocked back on his heels. She could see the tension in his jaw. "I was working at the Bar M right alongside R.J. Being together like that, day in, day out… We got real close. For the first time in my life, I thought maybe just maybe, we were building toward something real. Something lasting. A local television crew was coming to do a feature on the Bar M. He promised me I'd be part of it, that he'd introduce me as his son. He said I'd be standing right there next to Jane and Roger Jr. I felt so blessed to finally be acknowledged. It was like this huge cloud lifted and the sun was bursting through."

He shuddered, his whole body heaving with the effort. "Mama tried to warn me. Told me he wouldn't follow through."

He hung his head, focusing on the ground as he drew circles in the dust with the toe of his boot. A wild chuckle burst from his lips. "On the day of the shoot, he pulled me aside and told me he couldn't go through with it, that his wife wouldn't let him publicly acknowledge me. He said it would hurt his other children. I left that day and never went back. I haven't seen him since… Not till this evening."

"Not once in six years?" She couldn't hide the shock in her voice.

Although Dylan had told her about being estranged from his father, she'd had no clue about the reasons. The circumstances behind it were devastating. Again and again, his father had wounded him, and even when he'd given him another opportunity to get it right, he'd broken his promise and shattered the last vestiges of Dylan's belief in him. She felt a strong urge to turn back around and give R. J. McDermott a piece of her mind.

"Not once. Not a call or a letter or an email. He tried to reach out to me, said he wanted to make things right, but I wasn't interested. Not after what he did." His voice sounded raspy, and she sensed he was fighting against a tide of emotion.

"Do you think there's any way the two of you could—" she began.

"No," he said sharply. "Too much water has passed under that bridge. I'm not some little kid looking for his father's love and approval."

She wanted to remind Dylan about what he'd said to her about forgiving her mother, but she stopped herself. The situation wasn't the same, not by a long shot. Dylan had suffered a lifetime of not feeling good enough due to his father's actions. Over and over again, he'd been hurt. That wasn't a simple fix. There were so many layers to the situation, so many undercurrents swirling around.

As she drove back to the ranch, she couldn't help but

notice the strained vibe between them. Dylan's body language had closed him off. He sat in the passenger seat and stared out the window. A few times she tried to make light conversation, but he wasn't giving her anything more than monosyllabic answers. When they arrived back at Horseshoe Bend Ranch, Dylan saw her to the door, then brushed a quick kiss across her forehead. She stuffed down her feelings of disappointment that the kiss wasn't as romantic as she'd hoped for. In a perfect world they would have sat down together on the porch and held hands or kissed underneath the stars.

When Dylan headed off into the night he didn't once look back at her. She willed him to turn around, to give her one last, lingering look to let her know that nothing had changed between them. There was no look, nor a goodbye wave as he heaved himself into the truck and started its engine. A chill ran down her arms as his truck roared off into the onyx night, leaving her staring after him with a strong sense of foreboding settling over her.

Chapter Eleven

I'm not going anywhere, Dylan. Not until we can hash things out.

His father's parting words had thundered in his ears all through the night, resulting in a fitful sleep. He'd given up trying to get some shut-eye, knowing his turbulent thoughts would keep him awake. The simple truth was he didn't want to hash anything out with his father. He didn't want to listen to what he had to say.

Why not? a little voice inside him nudged. *What are you afraid of? That you still care? That you still have love for him even though you don't want to? That he still has the power to make you feel like that wide-eyed child who cried his eyes out when Daddy didn't show up on Christmas morning?*

He shrugged off the torturous thoughts as he headed toward the ranch for a full day's work. West Falls had been his safe haven, his brand-new shiny start. Now it had been tainted by his father's unexpected arrival. More and more as of late, he'd begun to like the man he was becoming. A man who wasn't bogged down by past disappointments and family dysfunction. A man who knew that his worth wasn't determined by his last name.

Right now he felt as confused as he'd been six years ago. In the span of a few minutes in R. J. McDermott's presence, all his confidence had been shattered. All his doubts had returned. About himself. And his father. And Holly. A half dozen times last night, he'd had to stop himself from throwing his things into a suitcase and taking off for parts unknown. The only thing stopping him was Holly. He owed her more than that. More, probably, than he'd ever be able to deliver.

She didn't deserve to pin her hopes and dreams on someone like him. Cullen's image popped into his head. Solid, dependable Cullen. He was a deputy. He was part of the fabric of this town. Her brother's right-hand man. A man like Cullen wouldn't disappoint Holly. He'd be as sturdy as a brick wall.

It wouldn't be fair to lead Holly on without knowing for certain if he could go the distance with her. Memories of his mother came into sharp focus. Her face puffy from lack of sleep. Her eyes red rimmed from crying. All because she'd never gotten over loving his father. Pain seared through him at the notion that he could inflict such damage on Holly. *Like father, like son.* Hadn't that always been his worst fear?

Spunky, amazing Holly. She was too good for him and the uncertainty that plagued him. She didn't deserve to be with someone who was filled with so much indecision. After all she'd been through, he couldn't be the person who hurt her. He wouldn't! It was far better to slightly wound her now than to devastate her further down the road. As loving as she was, he knew it was only a matter of time before she surrendered her heart to him. If she hadn't already.

All morning he kept himself busy at the ranch. He spent hours working with the Angus cattle in the southern pasture. And when he was done, he went straight to work on a project in the stables. Around midday he caught sight of Holly in the corral, having her lesson with Malachi, but he didn't venture outside to watch. After last night, he didn't have the slightest idea how to get things back to normal. He still felt so off-kilter, with his mind racing in a hundred different directions. He was afraid she would see the uncertainty in his eyes and call him on it. How could he tell her everything that was bottled up inside him?

After her lesson, Holly sought him out as he was trimming Warrior's hooves. She kept a respectable distance until he was finished. Having grown up around horses, Holly knew all too well the dangers of startling a horse.

"He's really taken to you," she said once he'd finished the job.

"I think he likes having my undivided attention," he answered as he rewarded Warrior with a sugar cube. "Haven't met a horse yet who didn't like to be pampered a little bit."

Within seconds, the conversation between them stalled out. The silence between them was weighty. Holly kept casting him curious glances, as if she was trying to figure something out. And he couldn't seem to find his way back to that comfortable, easy rapport they'd established. He kept wanting to look over his shoulder to make sure his father wasn't going to show up and shatter the sweet peace he'd found.

Holly frowned at him. "You seem a million miles away from here."

He tried to smile at her in an attempt to lighten the mood, but his mouth didn't seem to want to cooperate.

"What are you talking about? A man can't be in two places at the same time," he said, trying to make his tone sound light.

"Something's changed in you since last night," she said in a quiet voice. "You haven't been the same ever since you ran into your father."

He shot her a questioning look. Was his mood that heavy? Was there a dark storm cloud hovering over his head?

She continued, "You seem somber. Distracted. And right now you just seem to be going through the motions."

He bowed his head. It was already happening. He could tell by the wounded tone in Holly's voice that she was hurt by his behavior. Confused about his moody temperament. Disillusioned. Pretty soon everything would fall apart. Everything was slipping away from him.

"I'm sorry if I'm disappointing you." And he was sorry. More than he could put into words.

Holly met his gaze, her eyes flashing with surprise. "You haven't disappointed me. I just wish you'd let me in. I know you're hurting. I know your father showing up knocked you off balance. But you're holding it all in. I thought we could talk about anything." She let out a sigh. "In our letters we always managed to cut through everything and get straight to the important stuff. Has that changed?"

He didn't know how to answer that question. Truthfully, with his father being in West Falls, it felt as if everything had changed. How could he put it all into words and make her understand?

"Holly, I'm not sure you could ever see where I'm coming from. How I feel. Your whole life you've had this solid, intact family unit. Me, I don't know what a real family is. What it looks like. Seeing my dad just reminds me of what I am, where I come from."

Holly shook her head fiercely. "Your mother was your family, Dylan. And she did a wonderful job raising you, despite all the financial hardships, the gossipmongers and being a single mother."

"Yeah, she did," he said with a nod. "But my father—he bailed on us. Me, especially. I have no idea what it's like to have a father, one who puts you first and loves you unconditionally. He didn't even give me his last name. You have no idea what that does to a person."

She looked stricken, and her cheeks were flushed crimson. "No, I don't know. I can't imagine how much pain you've gone through. To tell you the truth, it hurts me to even think about it. But what I do know is that you can't let your past determine your future."

"But what if I'm like him, Holly? What if I bail on you when things get tough?" He turned toward her, seeking an outlet from all the turbulent emotions he was waging war against. "I don't want to ever hurt you like that. I don't ever want to be the one to cause you pain. I can't let that happen!"

* * *

Fear trickled along her spine. The intensity in Dylan's voice was causing warning signs to flash before her very eyes. He sounded so unsure, as if he were precariously straddling a fence, with no certainty as to which side he might land on.

Suddenly, she felt as if everything was slipping away from her. Every dream she'd nurtured for herself and Dylan hung in the balance. And there was nothing she could do to change things. He was wavering. He was backing away from what they'd built. She could hear it in his voice. It shimmered in his eyes and in the way he looked at her. Her heart sank into her belly.

In some ways she'd always expected this. Ever since Dylan had arrived in West Falls, she'd been dreading this moment. He'd always been just out of reach, like a high-flying kite she'd never been able to hold on to. So far she'd been savoring all the precious moments they'd shared, just in case things didn't work out the way she hoped. Instead of prolonging the agony, she wanted to cut to the chase. It was always better to rip off the bandage rather than to tug at it, bit by bit. Either way, she knew it was going to be unbearably painful.

"What are you saying?" Her mouth felt as dry as sandpaper, yet she somehow pushed the words out. "It's best if you just spit it out."

Dylan raked his fingers through his hair. "I stayed up last night, thinking this through." Dylan's eyes were bleak. Empty. "I'm going to be moving on from West Falls."

"Moving on?" she asked dully. Had she heard him right? "But I thought—"

She swallowed painfully. Her tongue felt heavy. What had she thought? That Dylan would stay in West Falls forever? That they would ride off into the sunset together? That he would love her?

"I thought we were—" Her throat constricted as she tried to utter the words. Pride wouldn't let her finish her sentence.

"I know. So did I." He let out an agonized groan, and his tortured gaze swept over her. "I'm not the man you need. Don't you see, Holly? I'm broken. Seeing my father brought a lot of issues to the surface. It made me realize how unfair I was being to you. How can I promise you a future when I'm not even sure of anything myself? Coming face-to-face with him after all this time brings back all the doubts and insecurities. I thought I'd closed a door on that, but I haven't."

"I haven't asked for promises," she said in a quiet voice. She hadn't asked for anything from him other than his forgiveness. It still surprised her that he'd given it to her so freely. But the truth was, she wanted so much more.

Dylan was rattling off a string of excuses, each and every one sounding like a platitude. The bottom line was he didn't want her. And he wasn't sticking around to fight for the life they could have together. He was giving up. He was running.

Waves of pain washed over her. She pressed her hands against her belly as her insides roiled and twisted. Was this Dylan's version of "it's not you, it's me"?

"I know you haven't asked for anything, Holly. And you probably never would. You believe in people, and you give everyone the benefit of the doubt." A poignant smile swept across his face. "But you deserve promises…and commitment and devotion. I have no doubt you'll find those things."

"Just not with you." She choked the words out, almost against her will. Dylan locked gazes with her, and she watched as a tremor ran along his jaw. He seemed to be fighting some invisible battle. He opened his mouth, then shut it. He clenched his teeth.

A look of pain was etched on his face. He sucked in a deep breath. "I've got to go pack up my things and talk to Doc."

She now knew what it felt like to lose the love of her life. It was so much more incredibly painful than she'd ever imagined. Why hadn't she known it would be this awful, this devastating? Why hadn't she prepared herself for this possibility? How could she have allowed herself to get so wrapped up in loving him that she'd forgotten to wear her suit of armor? For so long she'd been shielding her heart, yet in one fell swoop, Dylan had torn down all her defenses and wedged his way into her very soul. And now she was going to lose him. She was going to have to live a life without him.

Dear Lord, give me enough strength to let go of Dylan with grace and humility. I love him more than words can ever say, but I know that doesn't give me the right to hold on to him. I have to love him enough to let him go and make a life for himself on his own terms.

She wanted him to stay. If begging would do the trick, she'd have done it, throwing her pride to the wind in the process. But what would she gain by having Dylan stick around out of pity? No, that was the furthest thing from what she wanted. He'd marked her, branded her very soul with his gentleness and goodness. Because of him she would never be the same. Despite her fear of rejection, she'd opened up her heart to him. She'd cast away all her fears and insecurities, all in the hopes of making a future with him.

And since she loved him—with every fiber of her being—she had to let him go.

"Dylan, I'm not going to beg you to stay. If something inside of you is telling you that a life in West Falls isn't the life you want for yourself, I have to respect that. From the moment I read your first letter, I wanted nothing but good things to come your way. And that hasn't changed one bit."

He reached out and swept his palm across her cheek, his fingers trembling as they grazed her skin.

"Will you—?" His voice broke off, swallowed up by emotion.

She knew instinctively what he was asking. "Don't worry about me. I'm going to live my life," she said in a strangled voice. "I'm going to stretch myself, to go after all the things I want to accomplish. Whether it's rock climbing or going on a plane by myself or carrying a child, I'm reaching for the brass ring."

He brushed his hand over his face and heaved a tremendous sigh. "Holly, you deserve all that and so much more. I wish I was the man who could make all your dreams come true."

He bent down and brushed a fleeting kiss across her lips. His lips tasted salty, and she realized it was her own tears, which had slid down her face onto her mouth. Bravely, she wiped them away. Before she knew it, he was walking away from her and out of the stables, disappearing from view within seconds. She steeled herself against the ripples of pain coursing through her body.

Loving Dylan was out of her control. Losing him wasn't something she'd ever wanted to face, although from the moment he'd arrived in West Falls, a part of her had always feared it would happen. But her life wasn't over. She still had miles and miles to go on her journey. In a few weeks, she'd be heading to Boston in order to meet one of the top specialists in the world. An unexpected phone call from the doctor's office had forced her to make a swift decision. She'd said yes to the consultation, knowing it would allow her to get the answers she needed. She was going to swallow her fear so she could create positive changes in her life. Although a part of her soul would always belong to Dylan, she loved herself enough to know she deserved happiness.

She was no different from Cassidy or Regina or Jenna. They all yearned for the same things. A family. Faith. Someone special to adore and be adored by. A soft place to rest their heads at night when the day was done. Cherished friends. She wanted it all. A life she would proudly live out for as long as she graced this earth.

Before Dylan had come into her life, she'd really not been sure what she could give back as a partner. Now she knew. She'd never really considered herself worthy of the happily ever after. In the back of her mind, there had always been a niggling idea that she wasn't wife material. But that was yesterday. In God's eyes, she was perfect. Now there were no more doubts about whether she was whole enough or whether her disability would be a burden. Real, lasting love saw past all that. Someone who loved her, truly loved her, wouldn't allow obstacles to get in his way. And she knew Dylan's doubts had nothing to do with her disability. It was about his feelings of self-doubt and his fear of following in his father's footsteps. He was tangled up in the past. He was stuck. She wasn't. Not any longer.

Dylan drew in a sharp breath as he made his way to his truck. An agonizing sensation seized his chest. He wasn't breathing normally. Everything was a blur. He didn't feel steady on his feet.

He'd just hurt the most wonderful woman he'd ever known, and even though he knew he was sparing her pain in the long run, it still gutted him to do it. The urge to turn around and run back toward Holly was overwhelming. Every step he took in the opposite direction caused him to physically ache.

He vaulted into his truck, revved his engine and drove away from Horseshoe Bend Ranch as fast as he possibly could. Maybe, just maybe, he could outrun the pain. That was what he was good at, wasn't it? Running. Instead of easing up, the hurt was intensifying.

Walking away from Holly might just kill me, he realized. Never in his life had he felt this overwhelming sense of loss. There was a twisting sensation in his stomach, threatening to double him over. He was battling a tidal wave of emotions. The urge to run away was strong. It was what he always did, wasn't it?

He didn't belong here! Holly was a vital part of this town. She was the all-American girl who everyone adored. He, on the other hand, was just a visitor passing through West Falls. So why did it feel as if his right arm was being chopped off? Somewhere along the way he'd become a part of the fabric of this town. Aside from Holly, he'd forged relationships with Doc Sampson, Malachi, as well as Frank and Maggie. And the ranch hands were quickly becoming some of his closest buddies. It killed him to think how deeply he'd wounded Holly. He'd seen the devastation and confusion in her eyes. It mirrored all the emotions he'd been at war with ever since his father had waltzed back into his life.

As he reached the cottage, he parked his truck and got out. For a few minutes he stood in front of the door, not fully understanding why he couldn't force himself over the threshold. He stalked back toward his truck, then retreated a few paces. He continued to walk back and forth between the cottage and his truck, his mind whirling with a hundred different thoughts.

Despite all he'd accomplished in his twenty-seven years, he still didn't feel good enough. That was what this was all about. The wounds were still there, just under the surface, always ready to creep back into existence. The childhood he'd experienced could never be undone. And the scars would carry over into his relationships—his ability to fully commit, to believe in the durability of love.

All this time he'd thought his doubts were about Holly. But in actuality, they had always been about him. His past. His fears. His running away. His doubts about being able to fully love a woman for the long haul. The legacy he'd inherited from his father.

He sat down on the front stoop. Wasn't it time he dealt with it? He was tired of running, and he was emotionally exhausted. It was one thing when his past caused him pain, but now it was hurting Holly, as well.

And he didn't have to run away from West Falls to know that he couldn't breathe properly without her. He couldn't think straight, couldn't smile, laugh or do much of anything. Without her, he wasn't complete. There was a big, gaping hole in his life without Holly in it.

He was in love with Holly Lynch. The knowledge came sweeping over him like a strong gust of wind. Over-the-moon, can't-stop-thinking-about-her, soul-shattering love. He could try to push away those feelings for all eternity and they would still be there, nestled around his heart like a vise.

He loved Holly. He would always love her. She was a beautiful, healing balm. The letters she'd written to him had turned his whole life around. She'd strengthened his faith and given him the strongest motivation possible to survive Afghanistan. She soothed his soul in a way no one else ever had. There was no one else who would ever be able to, he imagined. Holly made him laugh out loud. She'd brought him closer to the Lord and made him believe that all things were possible. Her humble spirit and giving nature made him want to be a better man.

And each time he looked into her soulful eyes, he saw every dream he'd ever wished for reflected back at him. He couldn't imagine finding all those things in another woman, not if he searched the whole world over. And running away from West Falls, away from Holly, wouldn't change the way he felt. A home. Kids. A woman who would stand by his side, come what may. The possibilities were endless.

He heard someone calling his name. Doc was standing there, staring at him with a furrowed brow and a bewildered expression.

"Son, are you okay? I got your message that you needed to see me immediately. Is something wrong?" Doc's gravelly voice was laced with worry.

He'd completely forgotten that he'd left a message at the diner for Doc. A few hours ago he'd had every intention of giving the keys to the cottage back to him and saying his goodbyes before heading out of West Falls. Now nothing could be further from the truth. He wasn't going anywhere. It just wasn't possible. For the first time in his life, he knew he was planted right where he belonged. And he intended to let Holly know in no uncertain terms how he felt about her. As a feeling of euphoria washed over him, he reached out and clapped his hand on Doc's shoulder. His hand landed more forcefully than he'd intended, causing Doc to jump a little.

"I'm good." He threw back his head and let out a cackle of laughter. "No, I'm better than good. I'm great. Fantastic, actually."

Try as he might to contain it, he was acting like a giddy fool. And even though he was slightly embarrassed, the other emotions he was feeling were way more important.

Doc cocked his head to one side and studied him. "Dylan, was there a reason you wanted to see me? If not, I'm going to head back to the diner. I'm not sure Robin can handle the dinner rush all by her lonesome."

"Go on. Head back to the diner. I've got to drive back to the ranch and see Holly."

Pure adrenaline was racing through his veins. He suspected that a silly grin had popped up on his face.

Doc nodded. "Okay, then. If you're sure you don't need me. I'll see you later."

Doc walked away and headed down the street toward the Falls Diner. He cast a few curious glances back in Dylan's direction.

Dylan waved at him and jumped into his truck, full of fire to get back to Holly. All of a sudden his palms began to moisten as he gripped the steering wheel. What if Holly didn't want to see him? What if he'd blown it? No, he wasn't going to get his head tangled up in negative thinking. He had to take action! He had to make things right with her before the sun went down on this day. As he made his way back toward Horseshoe Bend Ranch, he prayed that he hadn't burned any bridges he couldn't rebuild.

Chapter Twelve

Holly sat in the stables, watching as the sunset dipped down beneath the horizon. A riot of colors lit up the sky. Oranges, pinks and purples. For the past few hours she'd been putting off heading back to the house. It would soon be nighttime, and once this day was done, Dylan would be out of her life. She'd wake up tomorrow morning to the stark reality of his absence. And even though she was willing herself to be strong, her body trembled at the daunting task stretched out before her. How would she manage to carry on without falling apart at the seams?

Count your blessings. She'd grown up hearing those words roll off her mother's tongue. She and Tate used to joke about how frequently that sentiment was ingrained in their minds. Although she knew it was true, she was having trouble practicing it at the moment. Try as she might to stay positive, her head was pounding with tension while her thoughts were jumbled and chaotic.

Over time she'd really grown to believe that she had a future with Dylan. *Fool,* a little voice whispered. Fool for believing in happily ever afters and fairy-tale endings. It worked out that way for some people, but not for her.

She heard a rustling sound behind her. It sounded like cowboy boots crunching against the wood floor. *Malachi.* She couldn't face him. He'd see it all on her face in an instant, the same way he always did. It was too soon to share her sorrow. She wasn't ready to tell anyone yet. She ducked her head down, determined to avoid eye contact with him. There would be time later to tell him Dylan was gone.

And Tate, also. Although he wasn't an I-told-you-so type of person, she still cringed at the prospect of having to broach the subject with her overprotective brother. She raised her hands to her mouth as a tight, familiar sensation gripped her. She had to stop herself from crying out. Loss. It made her whole body ache. Having been down this road before, she knew the loneliness and pain that awaited her. The endless nights between darkness and dawn where nothing could fill the void. The very thought of it made her clench her fists at her side. Once again, she'd have to be as strong as granite, even when it felt as if her world was spinning out of control.

"Holly." The deep pitch of the voice surprised her. She whirled her chair around, her eyes drinking in the sight of Dylan. He was standing a few feet away from her, his short dark hair tousled, a sheepish expression on his face as he gazed at her. For a moment her mind went blank. Why was he here? Wasn't he supposed to be on the road, hightailing it out of West Falls? Wasn't he supposed to be gone?

She said the first thing that came to mind. "Did you forget something?"

He nodded his head. "Yes, I did. I forgot you, Holly."

"Wh-what are you talking about?" Had she heard him right? He'd forgotten her?

He moved toward her, reaching her side in seconds. His eyes skimmed over her face with a look of such tenderness it robbed her of the ability to speak. She had so many questions sitting on the tip of her tongue, but she couldn't give voice to any of them. All she could do was stare at Dylan. She'd truly believed that she would never see him again. He was smiling at her now, a full-on, gorgeous, pearly-toothed smile, which reached right into her chest cavity and tugged at her heart.

"For a little while there, I forgot about us. About what you mean to me, what you've always meant to me. I forgot that running away from my problems has never worked out in the long run. And I forgot how very much I love you."

I love you. Three little words, spoken with such tenderness. And conviction. The raw intensity in his voice brought tears to her eyes. But a little while ago, he hadn't been so certain. He'd been on the verge of walking away from her, hadn't he? How could she believe in this when she'd come so close to losing him?

"I see the confusion on your face, and I don't blame you one bit. A few hours ago I walked away from you, and now I'm back telling you that I'm in love with you." He reached out and clasped her hand. "But it's true. I love you, Holly."

She pulled her hand away from him, needing to focus on her feelings rather than get swallowed up by the emotion of the moment. More than anything in the world, she'd wanted this declaration of love from Dylan. As their relationship had developed, she'd dreamed of a moment like this. She'd hoped and prayed for it. Having him here in West Falls had served only to intensify her feelings toward him. He was everything she'd ever hoped for wrapped up in a rugged, handsome package. Brave. Kind. True. They shared the same values, and there weren't many men who cherished the land the way Dylan did.

But he was also still tormented by his past, so much so that it might affect their future. She needed to be certain Dylan's feelings were strong enough to pin all her hopes and dreams on. If not, how could they ever make it through the hard times that were sure to come their way? She swallowed past the lump in her throat. There were things she needed to say to Dylan if they were ever to move forward.

"I thought I'd lost you. You have no idea of what that felt like, what the past few hours have been like for me. It was the death of everything I've been holding close to my heart for the past year."

Dylan winced. "Holly, I'm so sorry for hurting you. As a man, I'm far from perfect. For a moment I faltered, and I let fear take over. But the truth is, I could never have left town, because the love I feel for you wouldn't let me." He let out a harsh laugh. "I didn't even realize it until I tried to leave. The weight of it hit me full force when I couldn't even bring myself to gather up my belongings."

His rugged frame shuddered. "No matter how I tried, I couldn't leave. Because it didn't make sense to be separated from the woman I love. And I do love you, so very much. It's been building up these past few weeks and months, but it wasn't until I got to know you up close and personal that I fell right over the edge. I got to see how truly amazing you are. My precious, courageous Holly. I'm completely, absolutely crazy about you."

His words were so humble and powerful. He was admitting his imperfections and his mistakes. He was laying it all out for her, warts and all. And he was telling her from the depths of his soul how deeply he loved her. She couldn't ask for more. Moisture stung her eyes as the full impact of his declaration washed over her. Finally, after all her years of wishing him into being, she'd found her other half.

"Dylan, I love you, too." She bowed her head as tears slid down her cheeks. "And I feel so overwhelmed to be loved by you. I'm so grateful that you turned your truck around and came back to me."

"I'm the one who's grateful. The day I received your first letter was the beginning of a whole new life for me." He squatted down so that they were near eye level. He brushed a lock of hair out of her eyes, then reached for her hand again. This time she didn't pull away. She squeezed his hand tightly. At this rate she might never let it go.

She bit her lip, feeling conflicted about shattering this perfect moment. "Dylan, you have to promise me something."

He lightly caressed her palm, his huge smile highlighting the dimple in his chin. "Anything, beautiful. You know that."

"You have to try to broker peace between you and your father." Dylan immediately tensed up and pulled away from her. He let out a low groan. Abruptly, he turned his face away from her. She reached out and grasped his chin, slowly turning his face back toward her. "I'm not saying you have to forgive him. That's between you and God. But in order to move forward, you need to get your house in order. You need to tie up all the loose ends, otherwise our future together could be clouded by everything you're holding on to."

Dylan frowned at her. A slow hiss escaped his lips. "You're right. I know you are. It's hard to move forward when there are still things from the past I'm conflicted about."

"So you'll do it?" she asked. She was almost holding her breath in anticipation of his response. There were mountains standing between Dylan and his father, but she truly believed reconciliation was possible. In her own life she'd reconciled with Cassidy after not speaking to her or seeing her for eight years. And she'd managed to forgive her mother for keeping Cassidy's letters from her. Deep down, Dylan loved his father, and she suspected R. J. McDermott loved his son, otherwise he wouldn't have made the effort to find Dylan. Everything in her life had taught her that with love, all things were possible.

"I'll try my best to meet him halfway, to hear him out. I'm not making any promises, but I'll give it a shot," Dylan said. His expression softened. "It won't be easy, but I've been trying to be a better man. I reckon forgiveness is a big part of that. It's a very humbling thought."

"All I ask is that you try. When and if you close the

door on your relationship with your father, you need to be at peace with it. I just want you to be at peace, Dylan."

The corners of his eyes creased as a slow smile began forming on his face. "When did you become such a wise woman, Holly Lynch?"

"I don't know. Maybe it was the day I decided to become your pen pal," she teased. "It forever changed both our lives."

Dylan raised his head and delivered a quick kiss to her forehead. "I'm so very thankful that God placed the two of us in each other's paths. I promise never to take our love it for granted again."

She shook her head and smiled. "Nor will I. We're truly blessed, aren't we?" She leaned forward and placed a sweet, triumphant kiss on Dylan's lips. He reached out so that his palms could cradle both sides of her face as the kiss deepened into one of pure celebration. As the kiss ended, Holly murmured his name, rejoicing over the love she'd found with her cowboy soldier.

Epilogue

~❦~

Three weeks later

The stack of letters was sitting on her bedside table when she woke up in the morning. Her mother had promised weeks ago to find the letters from Cassidy she'd hidden up in the attic all those years ago. There were twenty-one letters in all. One by one, she read the entire stack. Some made her laugh out loud, while others made her shed a few tears. Over the years the letters dwindled down to almost nothing. No doubt Cassidy had gotten the message loud and clear after not hearing back from her. She was so thankful her mother had saved them. In all those years Cassidy had never really left her. She'd been there in spirit, if not in body. That knowledge filled her with such hope. Even when things seemed darkest, the dawn still came.

God had given her that message when Dylan had showed up at Horseshoe Bend Ranch with his heart in his hands. In the end, love was stronger than fear and self-doubt. It trumped every other emotion known to man. She felt so very blessed to be this cherished. Life had never been so good. The very last envelope was a pretty blue, the color of a robin's egg. The handwriting that spelled out her name belonged to Dylan. She would recognize the graceful slope of his script anywhere. Careful not to tear the envelope, she lifted the flap, then gently pulled out the stationery.

She took the letter and pressed it up to her nose, relishing the woodsy, rugged scent. She hadn't realized how much she'd missed receiving Dylan's sweet, endearing letters. Her heart began to beat a little faster as her eyes scanned the page.

Dear Holly,

The simple act of writing your name down on this piece of paper makes me realize how much I've missed writing to you. All those weeks and months when I was in Afghanistan, and at this very moment as I'm putting these words to paper, I feel such a deep connection to you. Mere letters written on a piece of paper cannot express the depth of what you mean to me. I'd like to tell you with words while gazing into your eyes what you've brought into my world. I'm not sure if there are enough words in the English language to do it justice, but I'd like to try.

Please meet me at noon at this location—31 Trinity Pass Road. Just past the covered bridge.

With all my love,
Dylan

Holly pressed the letter against her chest, heaving a sigh at the beauty of Dylan's sentiments. Her heart was thumping wildly in her chest. After everything they'd been through, the letter deeply resonated with her. Dylan had changed her world in so many amazing ways. He'd made her realize that she was capable and resilient and worthy of her own happy ending. And by loving her, he'd restored her faith in a bright future.

As her GPS navigated her toward the destination, she began to wonder where this journey was taking her. There was nothing out here but wide-open spaces. She came upon a stone entrance with a hunter-green placard announcing it as 31 Trinity Pass Road. Turning into the driveway, she rode for about half a mile until she spotted Dylan standing next to a stone house, with Leo cradled in the crook of his arm. She drew in a deep breath at the sight of him.

Dylan waved to her, and she beeped her horn at him in response. She parked in the makeshift driveway, maneuvering her wheelchair and then herself out of the driver's seat with more speed than usual. Her curiosity was spurring her on. Why in the world had Dylan invited her all the way out here?

"Thanks for coming," Dylan said with a welcoming smile as she wheeled herself over to his side.

"Of course," she said. "Your note piqued my curiosity. I was counting the minutes down till noontime."

Dylan placed Leo down on the ground and moved a step closer toward her. "Holly, I've never really had a place to call my own. In Madden I always felt not good enough. Even though it was my hometown, I never felt a sense of belonging. Being the object of gossip and innuendo doesn't really lend itself to feeling accepted by the community."

Just thinking about Dylan's sense of isolation and lack of self-worth made her want to weep. It wasn't fair that he'd been made to feel unworthy and an object of scorn.

"I'm so sorry you went through so much," she said. It still amazed her how cruel people could be, particularly to a child.

"Being here in West Falls… It's allowed me to put all that behind me. I finally feel as if I'm home. And I wouldn't change the past, even if I could, because every step led me straight to you."

"Oh, Dylan," Holly whispered, her voice tight with emotion. "That makes me so happy."

"You've brought tremendous joy into my life. Before I met you, I was lost. Running away was how I dealt with feelings I didn't want to confront. I was so afraid of the past, so stuck on the painful things I endured that it was hard to believe I could find happiness. And I was terrified of not being strong enough to stay around. Growing up, I never saw any examples of true, enduring love. For me, it seemed like this elusive thing I could never grab hold of. You changed all that, Holly."

He lowered his head and brushed a sweet kiss across her lips. He stood back and looked at her, his eyes brimming with wonder. "What you've taught me—grace, humility, forgiveness. And most of all, resilience."

He reached into his pocket and pulled out a piece of rolled-up paper. He just stood there grinning at her, not saying another word.

She wrinkled her nose. "What is that?"

Dylan unfurled it and held it up for her to see. "It's the deed to this property. I own it."

She felt her eyes widening. "Dylan. Are you joking?" She choked out the words. He handed her the document and she ran her eyes over it, quickly scanning the deed proclaiming Dylan Hart as the owner of one thousand acres of prime Texas land. She swung her eyes up from the parchment so she could look at him.

"How?" There was no way in the world she could utter anything other than a single word.

Shock and awe had her in its grip. *Was this really happening?*

"R.J.… My father…wanted me to have something to call my own. He wanted to give me part ownership of the Bar M along with Jane and Roger Jr., but I told him I'd be sticking around these parts. He understood that I want to settle down in West Falls. Next thing you know, we're out scouting properties, and he's giving me a big fat check and calling it my inheritance."

Holly felt tears pooling in her eyes. "This is incredible. Not just the land, which is amazing in itself, but your reconciliation with your father. I knew the two of you were making progress, but I didn't dare hope for something like this. After everything that happened in the past, you've allowed yourself to try to forgive him. You're moving forward."

Dylan blinked several times. He seemed to steady himself against a swell of emotion.

"He offered me a huge olive branch. And he stuck around West Falls so he could try to bridge the gap between us. I couldn't ignore that or what it meant. In his own way, he loves me. At first, pride prevented me from seeing it, but I had to let go of the past and try to forge a new path with him. He was young and he made a lot of mistakes as a parent. I'll never forget how it feels not to have a father in my life and to not be acknowledged, but I do want to try to build a relationship with him. He says he wants to make amends. I want to be the type of man who can grant forgiveness. So we're going to work on our relationship, one step at a time. I want to move forward. I want to have faith." He gestured around him at the land stretched out before them. "I'd say this is a major step in the right direction."

As far as she was concerned, it was an excellent step toward healing and reconciliation. It was a grand gesture from his father, which would cement their future. Loving Dylan as fiercely as she did, she needed to make sure he wouldn't harbor any regrets.

"Are you sure you want to relinquish your ties with the Bar M? Your whole life you wanted to be acknowledged, to be part of the McDermott clan. Doesn't it feel strange to give up the opportunity to go back to Madden and take your rightful place at the family ranch?"

He leaned down and planted a light kiss on her forehead. His large palm caressed the back of her head, his fingers swirling through her hair. She closed her eyes, wishing she could make this moment last for more than a fleeting moment. So many things were changing for Dylan. His world was suddenly becoming a whole lot bigger and more centered. Was there still room for her in his life? Or would he soar away from her like a comet blazing through the sky?

"Holly, I'm not giving up a single thing. How could I be? All of my life I've been chasing a feeling. I wanted to belong somewhere, to have the sense of community you've had your whole life. I've been running in so many different directions, trying to fill up that hole, only to realize that you've already done that. From the moment I received your first letter, I knew in my soul you were meant for me. And when I first met you and I was filled with fear and second-guessing my feelings, my heart always recognized you. I'm so sorry I fought it for so long. But I promise you, the only place that will ever feel like home is where you are."

He reached into his jacket pocket and pulled out a sparkling diamond ring. She gasped as Dylan bent down on one knee and clasped her hand firmly with his own. He looked into her eyes, and what she saw reflected there caused tears to brim over her lids and trickle down her face. Deep in the darkest regions of her soul, she'd feared no man would ever look at her with such love and wonder in his eyes. She'd always worried that the accident had cost her a future with a loving man at her side. With one single gesture, Dylan had put all those fears to rest.

He reached out and brushed her tears away with his fingertips in a light caress that skimmed over her skin. "Holly, I want to be your husband. If you'll have me, that is. I've made a lot of mistakes with you. And I'm sure I'll make a bunch more over the years."

His eyes filled with tears, and his voice turned husky. "But if you'll agree to be my wife, I promise to be by your side for the rest of our days, loving and honoring you. I want to be that person you lean on when you get weary and the road becomes a little bumpy. And I want to lean on you, too, Holly. Through everything that life has in store for us, I want you to take the journey with me."

So many emotions were coursing through her. Joy. Hope. Disbelief. But she needed to make sure he understood the realities of her everyday life before he made any pledges. She had to be certain that he wasn't looking at their future with rose-colored glasses.

"Dylan. You need to know a life with me isn't going to be easy. There will be so many challenges, so many ups and downs. And my daily regimen of medication, all the physical therapy and doctor appointments. And I still may never be able to conceive a child, let alone carry one to term. It's possible, but not a given. I know how much you want children in your future."

Dylan reached up and pressed his lips against hers, silencing her in an instant. His lips moved over hers with conviction and certainty. When he pulled away from her, she saw everything shining forth in his eyes. Truth. Love. Forever. Everything she'd always dreamed of having.

He brushed his hand across her temple. "A life with you is all I've ever wanted. If you're willing to take this journey with me, you'll make me the happiest man alive. I think I've known you were my future from the moment I read your very first letter. And I know it won't be easy at times. I know we'll face challenges other couples don't have to worry about. But I believe in us, Holly. And there's no other woman I'd want by my side other than you. I want to prove myself to you, every day of our lives, from this moment forward."

She reached out and placed a finger over his lips.

"Shh. You've already proved yourself. By coming back to me. By being here, right by my side. By loving me."

He cradled her face in his hands. "Holly Lynch. My pen pal. My best friend. My other half. Will you do me the honor of becoming my wife?"

"There's nothing in this world I want more," she answered as she wiped away tears from her cheeks. "And there's nobody I'd rather go through life with than you. My cowboy soldier."

Dylan placed the diamond ring on her finger, letting out a "Hallelujah" when it fit perfectly.

Holly tugged at his collar and pulled him close enough that she could show him her gratitude for all the joy he'd brought into her life. Her lips brushed against his in a wonderful celebration of the love they'd found and everything their future held in store for them. They both knew with a deep certainty that their love was enough to weather all the storms, come what may.

* * * * *

Dear Reader,

I hope you enjoyed reading *Heart of a Soldier*. Writing Holly and Dylan's story was a privilege for me as an author. I had a lot of fun crafting their romantic journey. Since the moment Holly appeared as a secondary character in *Reunited with the Sheriff*, I wanted to create her love story. After everything she'd been through, it was pretty clear she deserved her happily ever after. And I think she found it with her handsome soldier-cowboy, Dylan.

Love—true, enduring love—is not limited to physically perfect people. Holly demonstrates an ability to triumph over adversity with faith, family and a strong sense of self. She has her moments of self-doubt, but in order to overcome them she draws strength from her firm foundation. Although Dylan is a model of physical perfection, his inner scars are deep and profound. More than anything, he craves enduring love and a place to call home. He finds those with Holly. Even though the journey might be tough, finding love is always worth the struggle.

I'm thrilled to be writing for the Love Inspired line. It's really been a dream come true for me.

I would love to hear from you, however you choose to contact me. I can be reached by email at scalhoune@gmail.com or at my Author Belle Calhoune Facebook page. I can also be found on Twitter, @BelleCalhoune, or at my website, www.bellecalhoune.com.

Blessings,
Belle

Questions for Discussion

1. Do you understand why Holly chose not to disclose her disability to Dylan in the letters they exchanged? What were her main reasons for not sharing this information?

2. Did Dylan jump the gun by showing up so unexpectedly in West Falls after more than a year of corresponding with Holly? Why? Why not?

3. Was Holly wrong to ask her best friend Cassidy to pretend to be her when Dylan arrived at the house? Did her request cross any lines of friendship?

4. Were you surprised when Dylan decided to stick around West Falls? How did his past affect his decision?

5. What were the things that grounded Holly during her recovery period after the car accident? What role did God play in her recovery?

6. What were the things that bound Holly and Dylan together? That pulled them apart?

7. In what ways did the roses support Holly? Was their friendship important to her overall journey?

8. Many of the characters deal with the issue of forgiveness. Who had the biggest journey toward forgiveness? Why?

A MATCH FOR ADDY
The Amish Matchmaker • by Emma Miller
Addy Coblentz and Gideon Esch are looking for love—just not with each other. But soon the unlikely pair discover their perfect match is right before their eyes.

DADDY WANTED
by Renee Andrews
When Claremont's wild child Savvy Bowers returns to care for her friend's orphaned children, she finds a home in the town she once rejected—and the man who once betrayed her.

HOMETOWN VALENTINE
Moonlight Cove • by Lissa Manley
Unexpected dad Blake Stonely needs a nanny—fast! When caretaker Lily Rogers comes to the rescue, can this caring beauty also mend his broken heart?

THE FIREMAN'S SECRET
Goose Harbor • by Jessica Keller
Fireman Joel Palermo has put his rebellious youth behind him. But when his return to Goose Harbor reveals his mistakes left Shelby Beck scarred forever, can he ever gain her forgiveness and her love?

HEALING THE WIDOWER'S HEART
by Susan Anne Mason
Seeking help for his troubled son, minister Nathan Porter makes a desperate plea to Paige McFarlane. But when her soothing words begin to heal his *own* heart, soon he's falling for the pretty counselor.

FALLING FOR TEXAS
by Jill Lynn
When teacher Olivia Grayson teams up with rancher Cash Maddox to keep his teenage sister on the right track, their promise to stay *just* friends is put to the ultimate test.

REQUEST YOUR FREE BOOKS!

2 FREE INSPIRATIONAL NOVELS
PLUS 2
FREE
MYSTERY GIFTS

Love Inspired®

LI13R

"Are you hurt?"

Dorcas froze. She didn't recognize this stranger's voice. Frantically, she attempted to cover her bare shins. "I'm caught," she squeaked out. "My dress…"

"*Ne, maedle*, lie still."

She squinted at him in the sunshine. This was no lad, but a young man. She clamped her eyes shut, hoping the ground would swallow her up.

She felt the tension on her dress suddenly loosen.

"There you go."

Before she could protest, he was lifting her out of the briars.

He cradled her against him. "Best I get you to Sara and have her take a look at that knee. Might need stitches." He started to walk across the field toward Sara's.

Dorcas looked into a broad, shaven face framed by shaggy butter-blond hair that hung almost to his wide shoulders. He was the most attractive man she had ever laid eyes on. He was too beautiful to be real, this man with merry pewter-gray eyes and suntanned skin.

I must have hit the post with my head and knocked myself silly, she thought.

"I can…" She pushed against his shoulders, thinking she should walk.

"*Ne*, you could do yourself more harm." He shifted her weight. "You'll be more comfortable if you put your arms around my neck."

"I…I…" she mumbled, but she did as he said. She knew that this was improper, but she couldn't figure out what to do.

"You must be the little cousin Sara said was coming to help her today," he said. "I'm Gideon Esch, her hired man. From Wisconsin."

Little? She was five foot eleven, a giant compared to most of the local women. No one had ever called her *little* before.

"You don't say much, do you?" He looked down at her in his arms and grinned.

Dorcas nodded.

He grinned. "I like you. Do you have a name?"

"Dorcas. Dorcas Coblentz."

"You don't look like a Dorcas to me."

He stopped walking to look down at her. "I don't suppose you have a middle name?"

"Adelaide."

"Adelaide," he repeated. "Addy. You look a lot more like an Addy than you do a Dorcas."

"Addy?" The idea settled over her as easily as warm maple syrup over blueberry pancakes. "Addy," she repeated, and then she found herself smiling back at him.

Will Addy fall for the handsome Amish handyman?
Pick up A MATCH FOR ADDY to find out!
Available February 2015,
wherever Love Inspired® books and ebooks are sold.

"What's wrong, Ella?" Josiah's dark blue eyes filled with concern.

Words stuck in her throat. She fought the tears welling in her. "My son is missing," she finally squeaked out.

"Where? When?" he asked, suddenly all business.

"About an hour ago at Camp Yukon. I hope you can help look for him."

"Let's go. My truck is outside." Josiah fell into step next to her.

Ella slid a glance toward him, and the sight of Josiah, a former US marine, calmed her nerves. She knew how good he was with his dog at finding people. Robbie would be all right. She had to believe that. The alternative was unthinkable.

He opened the back door for his dog, Buddy, then quickly moved to the front door for Ella. "I'll find Robbie. I promise."

The confidence in his voice further eased her anxiety. Ella climbed into the cab with Josiah's hand on her elbow.

As he started the engine, Ella ran her hands up and down her arms. But the chill burrowed its way into the marrow of her bones, even though the temperature was sixty-five.

Josiah glanced at her. "David will get plenty of people to scour the whole park. Do you have anything with Robbie's scent on it?"

"I do. In my car."

He backed up to her black Jeep Wrangler. "Where?"

"Front seat. A jacket he didn't take with him."

Josiah jumped out of the truck to get it before Ella had a chance to even open her door.

He returned quickly with Robbie's brown jacket in his grasp.

He gave it to Ella. "This will help Buddy find your son."

Ella leaned forward, staring out the windshield at the sky. Dark clouds drifted over the sun. "Looks like we'll have a storm late this afternoon."

Josiah's strong jawline twitched. "We can still search in the rain, but let's hope that the weatherman is wrong."

Ella closed her eyes. She had to remain calm and in control. That was one of the things she'd always been able to do in the middle of a search and rescue, but this time it was her son.

"Ella, I promise you," Josiah said. "I won't leave the park until we find your son."

Will Robbie be found before nightfall?
Pick up TO SAVE HER CHILD to find out.
Available February 2015, wherever
Love Inspired® Suspense books and ebooks are sold.

SPECIAL EXCERPT FROM

Love Inspired **HISTORICAL**

Newly returned Duke Caldwell is the son of her family's enemy—and everyone knows a Caldwell can't be trusted. But when Duke is thrown from his horse, Rose Bell must put her misgivings aside to help care for the handsome rancher.

Read on for a sneak peek of
BIG SKY HOMECOMING
by Linda Ford

"You must find it hard to do this."

"Do what?" His voice settled her wandering mind.

"Coddle me."

"Am I doing that?" Her words came out soft and sweet, from a place within her she normally saved for family. "Seems to me all I'm doing is helping a neighbor in need."

"It's nice we can now be friendly neighbors."

This was not the time to point out that friendly neighbors did not open gates and let animals out.

Duke lowered his gaze, freeing her from its silent hold. He sipped the tea. "You're right. This is just what I needed. I'm feeling better already." He indicated he wanted to put the cup and saucer on the stool at his knees. "I haven't thanked you for rescuing me. Thank you." He smiled.

She noticed his eyes looked clearer. He was feeling better. The tea had been a good idea.

"You're welcome." She could barely pull away from his gaze. Why did he have this power over her? It had to be the brightness of those blue eyes...

What was she doing? She had to stop this. She resolved to not be trapped by his look.

Who was he? Truly? A manipulator who said the feud was over when it obviously wasn't? A hero who'd almost drowned rescuing someone weaker than him in every way?

He was a curious mixture of strength and vulnerability. Could he be both at the same time? What was she to believe?

Was he a feuding neighbor, the arrogant son of the rich rancher?

Or a kind, noble man?

She tried to dismiss the questions. What difference did it make to her? She had only come because he'd been injured and Ma had taught all the girls to never refuse to help a sick or injured person.

Apart from that, she was Rose Bell and he, Duke Caldwell. That was all she needed to know about him.

But her fierce admonitions did not stop the churning of her thoughts.

Pick up BIG SKY HOMECOMING
by Linda Ford,
available February 2015 wherever
Love Inspired® Historical books and ebooks are sold.